Brian Padilla

MONKEY TROUBLE

Eva grabbed her knapsack and left the park. Lately nothing had been going right. She had pleaded for a pet, but her parents kept saying no. Eva wanted something of her own to love and take care of. What was so weird about that?

Eva kicked at the grass as she walked, head down and shoulders slumping. She didn't notice the rustling in the trees lining the path.

Suddenly a dark brown-and-black ball dropped right in front of her face. Eva stopped dead instantly.

The brown-and-black ball was all furry, but it wasn't like any animal Eva had ever seen up close before.

She stared at the mysterious creature as it dangled upside down from a branch and realized—

She was eyeball to eyeball with a monkey!

Books by Ellen Leroe

H.O.W.L. High
Heebie-Jeebies at H.O.W.L. High
H.O.W.L. High Goes Bats!
Monkey Trouble

Available from MINSTREL Books

Monkey Trouble

A Novel by
Ellen Leroe
Based on the
Screenplay by
Franco Amurri
and Stu Krieger

A
MINSTREL®
BOOK

PUBLISHED BY POCKET BOOKS

New York   London   Toronto   Sydney   Tokyo   Singapore

This book is a work of fiction. Names, characters, places, and incidents either are products of the author's imagination or are used fictitiously. Any resemblance to actual events or locales or persons, living or dead, is entirely coincidental.

A MINSTREL PAPERBACK *ORIGINAL*

 A Minstrel Book published by
POCKET BOOKS, a division of Simon & Schuster Inc.
1230 Avenue of the Americas, New York, NY 10020

Copyright © 1994 by New Line Productions, Inc.
All rights reserved.

All rights reserved, including the right to reproduce this book or portions thereof in any form whatsoever. For information address Pocket Books, 1230 Avenue of the Americas, New York, NY 10020

ISBN: 0-671-88740-8

First Minstrel Book printing March 1994

10 9 8 7 6 5 4 3 2 1

A MINSTREL BOOK and colophon are registered trademarks of Simon & Schuster Inc.

Printed in the U.S.A.

For my mother and father,
the source of creativity and humor

Monkey Trouble

CHAPTER
1

There was a party going on, and it was all happening at Venice Beach boardwalk in southern California. Girls with streaming hair shot by on in-line skates, while sunburned men jogged through the crowds, some chased by dogs. Bikers in rainbow-colored spandex wove in and out, dodging kids licking ice-cream cones. On this sunny afternoon, the smell of cotton candy, grilling hot dogs, and suntan lotion filled the air.

So did music.

Rock poured out of handheld radios. Someone strummed a guitar, while a group played the drums a few feet down the boardwalk. Tourists laughed and pointed at the different sights as they strolled along—until they came to the monkey. Then the tourists stopped.

A big crowd had gathered to watch the tiny brown-and-black monkey perform. Bright-eyed and furry-faced, he would run up to people and take their coins, tipping his hat to the men and bowing to the women.

His owner stood off to one side, playing "Pop Goes the Weasel" on a strange two-foot-long box that hung across his chest. The box was dark blue and decorated with curlicues. It made sounds like the organ music at a merry-go-round or a circus.

The man cranking the hand organ was strange as well. He looked just like a pirate, the kind that would smile as he ordered you to walk the plank. He wore a patterned bandanna, gold hoop earring, and a bright red military coat with fancy gold braid. He cranked the blue box and grinned, showing a mouth full of gold teeth. The monkey was pulling in lots of money on this mild, sunny day. The crowd clapped and smiled at the monkey's antics.

Two men in dark business suits at the back of the crowd were not smiling.

Charlie and Drake had a special reason to watch the little monkey at work. Drake put his expensive gold watch on Charlie's wrist. Then Charlie offered a dollar to the monkey. The monkey took the money from Charlie, jumped up into his arms, then scampered away. The monkey had taken the dollar bill—but he had taken Drake's gold watch as well!

Drake and Charlie nodded. The monkey had passed the test.

Charlie hurried over to the pirate.

"I need a word with ya, Pops."

The pirate turned his dark gaze to the stranger.

"Who's you? I'm busy."

Charlie leaned in close and dropped his voice. "Too busy to make fifty thousand bucks?" he asked.

The pirate immediately stopped playing his organ. He snapped his fingers to bring the monkey to his side.

"Show's over, folks!" the pirate announced.

Fifty thousand dollars! With that kind of dough he could buy himself a decent place and dump the tacky trailer he called home. Forget the house. He'd buy a car, some big, snazzy number to tear up the highway. Visions danced in his head.

He motioned, and the monkey jumped into his arms as he followed Charlie to the men's

3

car. Fifty thousand dollars! Hold on a minute, the pirate suddenly thought. This was sounding too good to be true. Who handed out fifty grand without a catch? Maybe Drake and Charlie were out to con him. He'd better keep his eyes open.

Walking a little more slowly now, the pirate followed Charlie to a black stretch limo. He let out an approving whistle. Talk about fancy cars! This one topped them all. The two goons were for real. No doubt about it. The pirate was about to say hello to the big time.

He settled into the jump seat of the limo with the monkey in his arms. He shook off the heavy hand organ and put it on the floor of the limo. Drake and Charlie faced him in the backseat. The pirate extended his hand for a handshake, but Drake waved him off.

"I want my gold watch," Drake growled, sticking out his hand. "Put it here."

The pirate nodded and picked up the hand organ. This part was kind of tricky. He couldn't let the two men see what he was doing. Covering up the organ, he touched a secret spot. A flap opened and the day's loot tumbled out. An avalanche of watches, jewelry, coins, and dollar bills was piled so high on the limo's black-carpeted floor that Drake's shoes were buried!

"Which one?" the pirate asked.

Charlie's jaw dropped. "Drake! This ape is a genius!"

"It's a *monkey*," the pirate snapped. "I'm the genius, not him. Shorty Kohn, most glad to meet you."

Drake pointed at the monkey. "Is it true you do burglaries with this little ape?"

"True?" Shorty snorted. "That's what we do best. Is that how I'm makin' fifty grand?"

"Let's talk about that later," Drake said. "First we want to see a demonstration, free of charge."

The limo pulled away into heavy traffic. The monkey crawled out of Shorty's arms and played with the hand organ. Charlie and Drake stared at the furry-faced monkey, but Shorty wasn't worried. After all, he had spent months training his monkey to be a thief and pickpocket. The little guy wouldn't let him down now. Shorty hummed under his breath while the monkey jabbed playfully at the organ keys.

The limo coasted down a quiet street in a nice, well-kept neighborhood. It stopped near an alley that ran behind an apartment building. The curbside door opened. Quick as a flash, the monkey hopped out, clutching an empty drawstring purse. Shorty watched him go with a proud, if rotten-toothed, smile.

The monkey scampered up a tree whose branches reached the building's upper floors. He stopped, waiting. Someone opened a window. Without pausing, the monkey climbed to a branch that reached the window and hopped onto the ledge. A man inside the bathroom flushed the toilet and left. The monkey jumped in, then made a face. What a stink! He lowered the toilet seat cover, then hurried to the door to listen. Who else was inside the apartment?

He heard the sound of a woman singing to a baby, and a man—the husband and father?—playing with them. The monkey had to be careful. He poked his head out of the bathroom door and looked around. No one in the hall. He took a few steps out and waited. Still all clear.

He scampered quickly down the hall and entered a big bedroom. He glanced around the room. What a lot of nice shiny objects, just the kind Shorty liked best. He darted to the dresser and picked up a small silver picture frame and a glittering antique diamond pin. He stuffed them into his cloth purse. He saw something else shiny and silvery. He popped it into the purse and then froze. Outside the room the man let out a huge sneeze.

Then the baby, a little boy about a year and a half old, toddled into the bedroom! The monkey dived under the bed, but he wasn't fast enough. With a squeal, the little boy grabbed his tail. Too late to escape. The monkey tried to wriggle out of the boy's grip, but the little boy held on. Together the two rolled under the bed, still wrestling with each other.

Down below a Jeep Cherokee pulled up in front of the apartment building. Nine-year-old Eva Boylan, all tousled gold-brown hair and flashing blue eyes, jumped out of the passenger side. She and her father, Peter Boylan, had been discussing her favorite topic: why she couldn't have a pet. Discussing, she thought with a snort. More like arguing. They always seemed to go at it on the weekends her dad had visitation rights. Her father, with sandy brown hair and the same flashing blue eyes, would patiently listen to Eva plead for a pet. Listen, and then calmly shoot down each of her arguments with his own.

Eva adored her dad, but she *really* wanted a pet.

"But, Dad, Katie has a dog," she said now. "Jesse has a dog. Catherine has a dog. Billy has a dog. Even Maya has a dog."

Her dad gave her his I'm-doing-this-for-your-own-good smile.

"So you can be special and *not* have a dog," he tried to joke.

"Very funny, Dad," Eva said with a sigh. She was beaten momentarily, but she wouldn't—*couldn't*—give up. She tapped the intercom button as her father finished cramming bits and pieces of her clothing into her weekend bag.

Just as the door buzzed open, a man walked out. A bulldog on a leash waddled beside him.

Eva's eyes lit up.

Talk about perfect timing! Maybe if her dad could see this wonderful dog, he'd realize how good it would be for her to own one.

She stooped down to pet the bulldog, who slobbered on her hand.

"Dad, look!" She beamed. "Isn't he adorable?"

About a pint of drool dripped from the dog's lips as he tried to jump Eva.

Her father saw the drool and not the dog. He rolled his eyes.

Eva stood up and jammed her hands into her pockets. Talking her parents into letting her have a pet was going to be harder than she'd imagined. But she wouldn't give up. This was going to be the week she'd change her parents' minds and finally own a dog.

Wait and see!

CHAPTER
2

Eva entered the noisy apartment with her dad and stopped in the hallway.

What a difference from her father's condo in Venice! Her father lived alone in comfortable and neat surroundings. The rugs were deep-pile white, the rooms light and airy, and you could hear yourself think. The apartment of her mother and stepfather, on the other hand, was noisy, cramped, and cluttered. Toys belonging to her eighteen-month-old brother, Jack, littered the floor. Framed finger paintings and baby pictures filled the walls. The TV set was tuned to some kids' program, and her mom, Amy, model slim and pretty, and her stepfather, Tom Gregory, were singing the "Itsy Bitsy Spider" song to Jack.

Just another Sunday afternoon in the Gregory house, Eva thought, before Tom stopped her and her father in the doorway.

"Hi, Peter. Come on in!"

Tom shook her dad's hand with genuine warmth. Tom was as tall as her dad, with dark brown hair and a friendly grin. He was so easy to get along with that you forgot sometimes he was a police lieutenant and could be tough— except when he backed up her mom about the messes Eva made or the sloppy state of Eva's bedroom.

Once she had a dog of her own, though, she'd show them all how organized and neat she could be. Eva had a plan about getting that dog, so she hurried right into her bedroom. She didn't stop to listen to her dad yak it up with Tom about how great their beach weekend had been. It *had* been great, but then staying at her father's condo in Venice was always fun. The two of them rode bikes together, went swimming in the ocean, or strolled up and down the boardwalk at Venice Beach.

Right now Venice was the last thing on her mind as she began coloring a picture at her desk. She had copied a rottweiler from one of the magazine photos of kids and dogs taped on the wall in front of her. A rottweiler was one of her favorites, because it was a tall and powerfully built black and tan breed. If you had one, you *really* had a dog!

As she colored in the grass at the rottweiler's feet, Eva sensed a movement behind her. It had to be her bothersome baby brother, always sticking his nose where he wasn't wanted. Too bad he couldn't read the sign on her door that stated No Jack Allowed. But that never stopped the little monster.

"Scram, Jack!" she snapped, without turning around.

The little monkey, not Jack, jumped at her voice and hurried into a hallway closet. What a mess! He hadn't bargained on so many people being in the apartment, and the little boy wouldn't let him out of his sight.

Searching for his furry friend, Jack poked his head into Eva's room.

"Are you deaf?" Eva said. "I said, stay out!"

Her brother blinked, then turned and left (no monkey here!) as Eva called, "Dad? I'm ready for you!"

Saying a little prayer (Please let this work!), Eva kissed her crossed fingers. When her father came in, she proudly showed him the colorful drawing of a man, a smiling little girl, and a very large dog.

Eva pointed to the little girl—"That's me." Then to the man—"That's you . . ."

"And who's this?" her father asked, frowning at the dog.

Eva flashed him her biggest smile. "That's our rottweiler, Dad. Best dog in the world."

Her father opened his mouth, then snapped it shut as he lowered himself onto a little chair next to his daughter. He thought for a few seconds before speaking.

"Eva, airline pilots don't have dogs. We travel too much."

"No problemo: When you're flying, he could stay here with me."

Her father lowered his voice. "Honey, how many times do you have to hear it? You can't keep a dog here."

Eva made a face. Her stepdad, Tom, had an allergy to animals. As much as she liked Tom, he was the main thing standing in her way.

"It's not my fault if he's allergic to animal hair," Eva said.

As if on cue, Tom sneezed—loudly enough to be heard from the living room.

"It's not his fault, either," her dad said.

"The only thing he's not allergic to is Mom," Eva complained. "And Jack," she added, wrinkling her face.

"Come on, be reasonable," Peter said. "If you want a pet you have to do it in stages. You start off with a clam, then a goldfish, then a turtle . . ."

". . . then a rottweiler," Eva finished triumphantly, pointing to the dog in her drawing.

Outside in the hallway, Jack had caught up to the monkey. Now he was standing in the bathroom doorway, blocking the monkey's only way out. The monkey faked a few steps toward the bedrooms. As Jack followed, the monkey dashed around him into the bathroom and disappeared out the window. Disappointed, Jack waved bye-bye.

The monkey scampered back down the tree and hopped into the waiting limo. He dropped the heavy purse into Shorty's outstretched hand. Shorty shook the purse and smiled. The monkey hooted proudly and jumped up and down.

Emptying the drawstring purse, Shorty dumped the loot onto the floor of the limo as it pulled away from the Gregorys' apartment building. Charlie and Drake eyed the antique diamond pin, a diamond ring, the silver picture frame, and a number of dollar bills.

"See? I told yous!" Shorty boasted. "I trained him to pick gold, jewelry, cash, silver!"

Drake smiled in agreement, then fished out a shiny nail clipper. He cocked an eyebrow at Shorty.

"It's a monkey, not an appraiser," Shorty said huffily. "So, what do you say?"

Drake leaned over to whisper in Charlie's ear. "This is perfect for the Marlow gig. Anything goes wrong, only a monkey'll be there to take the heat. He's got to love it."

"Who's 'he'?" Shorty demanded. "Just tell me what you need me to do. I won't let you down, I promise. What do you need me to do?"

"Take it easy," Charlie said. "First we got to run it by the boss."

"Charlie, let's give him a down payment," Drake said. "I have a hunch we're gonna do business with this guy."

Shorty beamed. Was his monkey talented or what?

Charlie stuck a hand in his right pocket but came up empty. He stuck a hand in the left pocket and still found nothing. Swallowing nervously, he began patting the inside of his jacket. Where was the money? Sweat popped out on his forehead. Drake scowled at him.

"I had it, Drake, I—"

Shorty checked his monkey's hands. Nothing. The monkey uncurled his tail: A wad of bills was hidden inside!

"Smart little guy!" Drake said with a laugh. "There's your advance, keep it!"

Shorty grabbed the money with a greedy laugh. That was a big wad of bills. Soon Drake, Charlie, and Shorty were cackling and laughing together. It wasn't a pretty sound. The monkey wrinkled his nose and clapped his hands over his ears. But Shorty ordered him to grind the organ. This was one big celebration, but the monkey couldn't get into the spirit of the thing.

CHAPTER

3

The Gregory family was gathered around the dining-room table later that Sunday night. Eva sat in her pajamas, nibbling at her dinner and thinking. Plan A of her Get a Pet project had failed. Her father hadn't liked her drawing of the rottweiler at all. Now it was time for plan B.

She turned to her mother.

"My school nurse said people can get over allergies. Sometimes having a dog around makes your body get used to it."

Amy was only half listening. She was sitting on the floor, changing Jack's diaper.

"Tom's allergy is not the only reason," her mother said.

Eva caught her stepfather's eye, then looked

17

away. Here it came, she just knew it. Another lecture about the responsibilities and duties of taking care of a pet. Her mother was big on the importance of responsibility.

"You're not responsible enough to care for a dog," Amy said. "You don't do anything I ask, your room is a disaster area, you never get anything done on time . . ."

Her mom finished diapering the baby, then offered the dirty folded diaper to Eva.

"Throw this in the kitchen, please," Amy said.

Eva sniffed the air in disgust. "No, *stank* you."

Her stepfather took the diaper into the kitchen and threw it in the trash, then began preparing a bottle for Jack.

Amy eyed Eva sternly. "If you can't even deal with a dirty diaper, how are you going to clean up after a dog?"

"Because I'd be doing it for my own puppy."

Tom came back in and handed Amy the bottle. She offered it to Eva.

"Here, do this for your own brother."

"Do I have to?" Eva said. "I'm eating. He can hold it himself."

"But a dog can't feed himself," Amy said. "You'd 'have to' do it twice a day."

Eva nodded. "I know."

"Would you give up watching your favorite TV shows when the dog had to be walked?" Amy asked.

Eva hesitated. That was a tough one. She stared down at her plate, not knowing what to say.

"Eva, listen . . ." Amy began.

There was something in her mom's tone that gave Eva hope. Maybe, just maybe, plan B was working. Eva gave Amy her most responsible look, the one that said, "I can do it, you just wait!"

"If you're so sure you can handle it, then convince us," her mom said. "Help out around here a little more, pick up after yourself . . ."

Bingo! Her mother *was* beginning to see her side of it. Maybe there'd be a pet in the Gregory apartment after all!

Eagerly, Eva began, "And then if I—"

But Tom cried, "Amy, look!" He pointed to Jack, who was silently doing the hand motions of "Itsy Bitsy Spider."

The moment was shattered. Her mother

rushed over to join Tom. Together they knelt by the baby, singing.

When they got to the part about the water spout, Eva pushed away from the table, an angry lump in her throat. "Down came the rain," she shouted, "and washed the brother out!"

Talk about dropping a bombshell, Eva thought, as Tom, Amy, and Jack stopped singing and stared at her in shock. No one understood. Eva ran to her room. She hooked the No Jack Allowed sign on the outside knob and slammed inside.

Trembling with anger, Eva stood there for a few seconds, then collapsed in a heap on the floor. Even though the door was closed, she could hear her mom and Tom singing the spider song to Jack. If she heard that dumb song one more time, she'd scream. She clapped her hands over her ears, she hummed loudly, but still she could hear them.

Then she heard the front door open and close. The singing had stopped. Eva took her hands away from her ears and listened. Her teenage cousin Tessa had come into the apartment and was greeting everyone. Personally, Eva often wondered what planet Tessa was from. All she ever talked about was rock stars and shopping malls, and one hand was permanently glued to *Rolling Stone* magazine. But Tessa had one bright spot to her Queen Flake personality: When she baby-sat for Eva and Jack, she never drooled over the little monster. Enough thinking about her baby brother. Eva threw herself onto her messy bed and began dreaming about rottweilers.

Later that night her mom came in to talk to her. Eva huddled under the covers, surrounded by her stuffed-animal collection. A cute stuffed monkey nestled close to her face.

Amy took Eva's hand. "Your brother loves you so much, Eva."

"Fine. I just don't want *you* to love him so much. You think everything he does is so . . . precious. I hate him, he's a nerd."

"Don't you remember how excited you got when I told you I was pregnant?" Amy asked.

"It sounded cool when Tom said I was getting a half-brother, but then a whole one showed up instead."

"Tell you what," Amy said. "Why don't I pack his bag right now. I'll leave him on the street tonight, and let's hope someone really nice finds him and takes good care of him."

As if they'd ever dump Jack out on the

street! Eva looked at her mom with a knowing grin. Amy smiled back at her.

Eva stifled a giggle. "Come on, Mom . . . just shoot him."

In a run-down trailer home in Venice Beach, Shorty Kohn was in the middle of his own conversation. He was talking to himself, though, and reading aloud from a letter. It was not a nice letter and not a nice conversation.

The monkey scampered up the wall of the trailer to get as far away from Shorty as he could. Now he was dangling upside down from a beam, just inches away from the angry face of his owner.

Shorty growled and reached for something on the kitchen counter. Splat! The monkey dodged a yogurt container as it sailed across the room. He jumped to the floor as Shorty kicked out blindly. A chair crashed against the wall.

Shorty's wife had just left him, taking their ten-year-old son, Mark, with her.

"She even took my freakin' food!" Shorty bellowed, staring into an empty refrigerator. The tacky trailer had been stripped clean— kitchen shelves, cabinets, and all.

The monkey scrambled atop the small kitchen table and peered at the envelope. Scratching his head, he stared at the scribbled lines that read "To Shorty." Then he listened to Shorty read aloud from the letter.

Puzzled, the monkey scampered into the bedroom area. The boy's bunk was empty, as was his closet and bathroom. All that was left was a dirty baseball cap and a photo of Mark scowling. Hurrying back to Shorty, the monkey held out the photo. Shorty glanced at the picture of his son, then angrily tore it up.

"The little jerk's gone. She left and took him with her—because of you," he said, glaring at the monkey. "She hated you and your stinking mess, and she hated me for keeping you around!"

Angry, Shorty kicked out at the monkey, who dodged the blow. Realizing he was in danger, the monkey hid inside the closet beside the boy's bunk. He had never seen Shorty so angry before.

At dawn the monkey crept out. All clear. Shorty was asleep on the bed, snoring loudly. Now was the time to escape. What had Shorty's wife done when she'd left? The monkey wrinkled his face, then hurried over to the messy kitchen counter. He found a piece of paper and a pencil and began scribbling wavy lines on it. He paused for a few seconds, peering at his work. Yes! It looked just like Shorty's letter from the night before. The monkey nodded and added a few more squiggles. Then he stuffed the paper inside the torn envelope and took off.

CHAPTER
4

Eva, come on, get dressed!"

Amy poked her head in the door and frowned.

Still in her pajamas, Eva kicked at the tangled mess of tights, socks, skirts, and sweatshirts on the bedroom floor.

"Everything looks disgusting on me."

Amy bent over and extracted a skirt, tights, sweater, and blouse from the jumble. "Do we have to do this every single morning?" she demanded. "You're already late, and you know Paul isn't going to wait. Look at this mess!"

She threw the outfit she'd assembled into Eva's arms.

"Now get moving. And I'm leaving the rest

of this stuff right here for you to put away when you get home."

Her mom yelled at her nearly every morning to get her act together, but today Eva realized her mother was only saying the words. Her heart wasn't in it. Something had happened. Amy's eyes were red.

"Mom, have you been crying?" Eva asked.

Her mother paused in the doorway, her face turned away from Eva.

"No, I'm just tired. I—I couldn't sleep last night."

Amy left the bedroom without telling Eva about the burglary of their apartment the day before. Not knowing about her mother's problem, Eva focused on her own: finding a decent outfit to wear to school.

Eva held up the sweater, blouse, and skirt her mom had picked out, then made a face. Too cutesy. Too gross, was more like it. Eva tossed the sweater and blouse on the floor, then discovered a crumpled T-shirt underneath the bed. Perfect! Now, what to wear with it? She pawed slowly through the mess at her feet.

Bzzz! Eva heard the intercom go off in the hallway. Paul, the twelve-year-old friend who walked her to school, spoke to her mother. "Mrs. Gregory? If she's not down in two minutes, I'm going without her." Eva heard every word—now she really had to hustle.

"Why do you do this to me?" her mother cried ten minutes later as she pushed Eva out the front door of the apartment building. "You knew Paul wouldn't wait for you, and now I have to walk you to school."

They rushed by the park, then approached the pet store. The pet store was one of Eva's favorite places. And Annie, the young woman who worked there, was one of Eva's favorite people. Eva could never resist stopping to gaze in the window at the adorable puppies. She had practically been running to keep up with her mother, but now she slowed down.

Amy shook her head. "Eva, that's enough! I said no!"

Just then Annie came out of the shop to set up a sign. "Good morning, Eva!"

Eva waved back, but her mom dragged her away. They'd really have to rush now to get to school on time.

Later that day Eva wished she had never shown up. It was her third grade's hour for show-and-tell, and little Miss Know It All Jesse had brought her Yorkshire terrier. She had even dressed it in a plaid sweater. Eva stared enviously at the very small dog.

"Well, this is my dog, Toto," Jesse began.

"Do you feed him?" Eva interrupted from her seat. "Do you walk him? Do you clean up his poop?"

At the mention of the word "poop," half the class broke into laughter. Katie, Eva's best friend, giggled the hardest. Even Christine, Eva's teacher, struggled to keep a straight face.

Everyone was laughing, but Eva had asked the questions seriously. You couldn't really say you owned a pet unless you took care of it yourself, right? Wasn't that what her mom was always drumming into her?

At the front of the class, Jesse wriggled in embarrassment.

"Well, actually, my mom does most of that stuff."

"Then he's not really yours," Eva declared.

"Wanna bet?" Jesse challenged her. "He is so mine."

"Only until your parents decide he's a big pain and get rid of him," Eva said smugly.

Jesse tightened her grip on Toto. "They're not getting rid of him!"

"Eva, please," Christine interrupted. "It's Jesse's time to talk. Do you want us to pay attention to you tomorrow when it's your turn?"

"Tomorrow?" Eva cried in panic. "I can't do it tomorrow! I forgot—I'm not ready."

"That's what you've been saying all month, Eva," Christine said. "You have to learn to be more organized, to follow a schedule. Go on, Jesse."

Jesse smirked at Eva and continued her talk.

Katie nudged Eva's arm. "Don't worry," she whispered. "You could always bring your brother."

"My brother?" Eva exclaimed in horror. "Yuck. Forget it."

That would be the day, when the little monster visited her third-grade class. Talk about major embarrassment.

Across town in a Venice Beach mobile home, Shorty's phone began to ring. The rumble of Shorty's snores drowned out the phone. The answering machine picked up.

"Shorty, this is Drake," growled a familiar voice.

At that Shorty jerked awake, opening bloodshot eyes. This could be the message he was waiting for.

"Looks like your monkey got a job," Drake continued. "Call me as soon as you get in. The boss wants to meet you."

Shorty sat up and cheered. All that time spent training his monkey was finally going to pay off. He'd pull off the one big robbery, and Shorty Kohn would be rolling in dough. No more playing a hand organ on the Venice Beach boardwalk.

Shorty whistled under his breath and got up. Life was certainly going to be different once he had money. For starters, he'd dump this depressing trailer and find a new home. Maybe hire a maid to pick up after him. He headed to the kitchen, stepping over chairs, yogurt containers, and empty cereal boxes. There might not be too much to eat for breakfast this morning, but coffee would get him going.

Shorty started searching for the kettle when he spotted an envelope propped on the table. It was addressed to him, in his wife's handwriting, but the message inside came from his monkey. Did those wiggly little nonsense lines mean what he thought they did? Had his monkey left him a goodbye note?

Mumbling under his breath, Shorty took two steps backward. He hit his head on an open cabinet door and cursed. If that furry little ape had left him . . . Shorty ran to check in Mark's room, where he stumbled over a chair. Jumping up and down and howling, he called out to his monkey.

No answer.

He was alone in the trailer.

Where in the world had the monkey gone?

CHAPTER
5

The monkey was moving fast.

He raced across rooftops, then darted down a fire escape and dived into a trash barrel. He buried himself under the garbage until he was completely covered. Safe at last! he thought. Or was he?

He peeked out. A woman in torn clothes bent over the barrel and stuck a hand in. Was she trying to grab him? No, she was reaching for a half-eaten banana. That would make a nice breakfast. The monkey snatched the banana right out of the woman's hand and pulled it down out of sight. He peeked out again. The woman's mouth was wide open. She backed away as if a Martian monster were chasing her. The coast was clear.

The monkey climbed out of the trash barrel and looked around. A pickup truck had stopped by the curb. Now was his chance to escape. Sticking close to the wall, the monkey edged to the street. The driver of the truck gunned the engine. Just as he took off, the monkey leapt onto the back of the truck. He jumped up and down in excitement. What a great day to go for a ride—and pick all the bits of garbage out of his fur.

Eva was having a great day too, playing basketball in the park with her class. It was a rough and tumble game, with a lot of shouting and shoving. Eva moved into position on the court, keeping an eye peeled on the basketball. She was really concentrating and playing extra hard. The ball was passed straight to her when Sally, from the other team, shoved her. Eva lost her balance and the ball. Of all the colossal nerve! She knew Sally had charged her on purpose.

Eva charged right back. No way would her team lose because Sally had cheated. Eva crashed into Sally, sending her tumbling to the ground. The coach caught this action and blew his whistle furiously.

"Boylan, what do you think you're doing?" he demanded.

Eva swung around to face the coach. "She shoved me first!"

"I did not!" Sally screamed. "I never touched her!"

"You did so, you liar!" Eva shouted.

"I did not, you troublemaker!" Sally said.

Sally grabbed the ball. No way was Eva going to let her get away with that. She hopped back on one leg and kicked the basketball out of the other girl's grip. It soared ten feet in the air.

The coach's temper soared, too. "All right, Boylan, that's it! Take a time-out!"

Muttering under her breath, Eva stormed off the court. Talk about unfair, she thought as she grabbed her knapsack and left. Lately nothing had been going right, nothing at all. She had begged and pleaded for a pet, and no one seemed to listen. They were all so caught up in other things—her mom and stepdad with the baby, her father with his job—that they didn't realize how important owning a dog could be. Eva wanted something of her own to love and take care of. What was so weird about that?

Eva kicked at the grass as she walked, head

down and shoulders slumping. The sounds of the basketball game were fading behind her, and she didn't notice the rustling in the trees lining the path.

Suddenly a dark brown-and-black ball dropped right in front of her face. She stopped dead instantly. Her knapsack slid out of her hands. Her eyes bugged out.

The brown-and-black ball was all furry—but it wasn't a cat. It wasn't a bird—it didn't have wings. It wasn't a squirrel—squirrels didn't hang by their tails. It wasn't like any animal Eva had ever seen up close before. She wanted to scream and run, but her feet were frozen. She stared more closely at this mysterious creature as it dangled upside down from a branch—and realized she was eyeball to eyeball with a monkey!

Its shiny black button eyes peered at her curiously. Then the monkey reached out and touched her Dodgers cap. He cooed, baring sharp front teeth that scared Eva even more. Before she could breathe, think, or move, the monkey dropped to the ground and hugged her knees. Feeling trapped, Eva raised her hands.

Luckily, just then a nicely dressed elderly couple strolled into view.

"Help, please . . ." Eva managed to squeak. "Help . . ."

Curious, the couple came over to Eva and the monkey.

"Oh, Harold, look at that little monkey!" the woman squealed. "Isn't it precious?"

The man beamed down at Eva. "That's quite a pet you got there, young lady." He turned to the woman. "Isn't that some pet, Kaye?" Then he said to Eva, "Does it bite?"

"I hope not!" Eva said.

The woman stroked the monkey. "He's so soft!"

Maybe the little guy isn't dangerous after all, Eva thought. She watched him lean against the woman as she stroked him, his little head twisting in pleasure. He was even making cooing noises, like a baby. Eva couldn't help smiling, and the monkey seemed to smile back!

As if to show how friendly he was, the monkey hopped right onto Eva's shoulder. She was beginning to like the furry little animal. Especially after he suddenly grabbed her Dodgers cap and stuck it on his head. You couldn't get a rottweiler to do that!

"Wherever did you get an adorable monkey like this?" Harold asked with a laugh.

Eva thought fast. "He . . . ah . . . in the Caribbean—from some pirates!"

"They still have pirates down there?" Kaye asked.

"Well, you know," Eva said with a wave of her hand, "retired pirates. They have a restaurant now."

"What's his name?" the man asked.

"His name?" Eva bit her lip. "Uh . . . Dodger! Because he likes the hat!"

The newly christened Dodger also liked the woman's earrings. They gleamed like gold, and he kept poking at them. Eva and the couple chatted and laughed at the monkey's antics as he hugged the man and then climbed onto the woman's shoulders.

He scampered off for a few seconds to play in the bushes. The elderly couple said goodbye to Eva and went on their way. Eva turned and found Dodger dragging her knapsack away. She had to laugh. The knapsack was almost twice his size. "Do you know you look like a monkey Santa Claus with a sack full of goodies?" Eva grinned. What was the little guy up to?

Just then two joggers ran past. Dodger nervously hooted and scampered behind a tree.

"Hey, you scared him!" Eva yelled at the joggers. "Dodger, are you all right?"

Walking slowly around the tree, Eva found the frightened monkey.

"Hey, little dude," she said in a comforting voice. "You're so cute! Did you run away from the zoo or the circus or something? Why did you come to me like that? My name is Eva. Do you need a friend?"

Like a dream come true, Dodger jumped straight into Eva's arms and wrapped an arm around her neck. Eva hugged him back, her eyes shut in sheer happiness. This was better than owning a rottweiler any old day!

"Okay, now you're mine," Eva whispered to Dodger. She slipped him into the knapsack.

But Eva hadn't counted on so many problems in trying to sneak Dodger into her building. First spaced-out Tessa and Jack brushed right past her out front. Jack pointed straight at the monkey, who had poked his head out of the knapsack. Eva's gum-chewing, magazine-reading cousin didn't see Dodger this time, but what about the next? And luckily for Eva, eighteen-month-old Jack hadn't yet said his first word. When he did, she prayed it wouldn't be "monkey."

Then the man who owned the bulldog

rushed to get in the elevator with them. At any other time Eva would have loved to play with the drooling dog, but not today. Not with Dodger jumping up and down in her knapsack. As the man and dog hurried to catch the elevator, Eva's knapsack began to do a tap dance all on its own as Dodger struggled to escape. Just as the elevator doors began to close, the bulldog stuck his wet muzzle inside. Eva bit her lip and pushed it out. She glimpsed the owner's puzzled face as the doors slammed shut.

Talk about a close call! But her heart nearly stopped when she stepped off the elevator on her floor. Police officers were walking out of her apartment just as she and her hidden monkey headed for the front door. Had her mom or stepfather found out about Dodger?

No, no one knew, she realized a few seconds later. The police and her mom didn't search her knapsack or ask questions about what had happened in the park. Hurrying into her bedroom, Eva assumed the police were there because of some connection with her stepdad. As long as they didn't ask her about that afternoon, she and Dodger were safe.

Eva unzipped the knapsack. Dodger instantly peeked out.

"This is my room," Eva whispered. "You can stay here with me, but we can't let anyone see you, or they won't let me keep you. You're my secret, okay?"

It wouldn't be too hard hiding a monkey in her room. Piles of clothes and shoes cluttered the floor. Toys, books, and stuffed animals covered the unmade bed.

"Eva?" Amy called from outside.

Dodger scooted under the bed a split second before Eva's mom poked her head in. Eva stood in the center of the room, innocently clutching a bundle of clothes.

"Good, you're cleaning up," her mom said with a surprised smile. "Want a snack or something?"

Too nervous to answer, Eva shook her head. The moment her mom left, the little monkey reappeared.

"Phew! That was close," Eva said. "I mean, if she had seen you—"

Suddenly Dodger darted to a corner and started running in tight circles. Eva stared at him in confusion.

"What's wrong? What are you doing? Are you trying to tell me something?" She paused, trying to guess. "You . . . ah . . . you . . ."

40

Dodger stopped running. When Eva looked again, there was a little puddle at his feet.

". . . need to go pee," Eva finished, a little too late. "Gross! Dodger, you can't do that!"

And she thought that baby Jack's bathroom habits (or lack of them) were disgusting! Dodger needed an instant dose of toilet training. After wiping up the mess with toilet paper, Eva shook a finger at the monkey. She had to admit, with his head hanging down he really did look ashamed.

"Bad, Dodger! Bad. No pee-pee on floor! Bad!"

It was time for potty training, and the sooner the better. Carrying Dodger into her private bathroom, Eva set her pet on the toilet seat and knelt right in front of him.

"Pee-pee here," she instructed with a phony smile. "Yes! Poo-poo here. Gooood. And then look . . ."

She demonstrated how to flush the toilet. The loud whooshing sound caused Dodger to leap into her arms. While she was trying to calm him, she heard her stepdad shout, "Eva? Katie on the phone for you!"

Oh no! Tom was in her room. She couldn't let him spot the monkey.

Eva dropped Dodger, kicked the bathroom door shut, and leaned against it.

"I'm in the bathroom," she cried. "I'll call her later!"

Dodger made the same running motions as before. Was he about to let loose again? Eva wanted to go to him, but she couldn't move away from the door.

"I've got the phone here, take it," Tom insisted from just outside.

"I can't, I'm on the toilet!" Eva shouted. She tried to motion Dodger to hop onto the toilet seat. "On the toilet!"

Eva could overhear Tom telling Katie she'd have to call her back when he let out a huge sneeze. Oh no, the monkey must be setting off her stepdad's allergies, she thought.

And then she got an even more unpleasant shock when Dodger stepped away from the toilet. He stared down at something in the bowl that made Eva hold her nose. Eva glared at Dodger, who scampered to flush the toilet. Oh brother, was this what toilet training was all about?

CHAPTER
6

In a run-down neighborhood across town, Shorty Kohn was making his own stink.

Only his was something he couldn't easily flush away.

Shorty had lost his monkey, and now he had to find him. That meant tracking down his runaway wife and ten-year-old son. The monkey had always liked Mark. Maybe he had followed Mark to this shabby rental house.

Checking the address on a slip of paper, Shorty climbed the rickety steps to the house and knocked on the door.

His son opened the door.

"What do you want?" Mark said with a scowl.

"Don't you dare talk to me like that," Shorty warned.

Mark glanced nervously over his shoulder and lowered his voice. "How did you find us? She knows you're here, she'll kill you."

"I'm not after her," Shorty said.

From somewhere in the house a woman yelled, "Who is it?"

"It's nobody!" Mark shouted back.

Shorty jabbed a finger in his son's face. "So now I'm a nobody?"

"You were always a nobody," Mark shot back.

Angry, Shorty lunged at Mark, who quickly dodged him.

"Where's my monkey?" Shorty demanded.

"You don't know?" Mark sounded really surprised.

The woman yelled again, "Who you talking to there?"

"I'm talking to myself!" Mark roared back.

Shorty took an impatient step forward. "Is the monkey here or ain't he?"

"'Course not. She'd never let me keep him around." Mark gave his father a look. "What happened, you lost him? I can't believe it! You lost him!"

44

"I didn't *lost* him, I just can't find him!" Shorty said.

Disgusted, Mark started to slam the door, but Shorty stuck his foot inside. Shorty knew he wouldn't win any Best Father awards, but he did care for his son. He dug into his pocket and pulled out an impressive wad of bills.

"Tell that ungrateful two-timing mother of yours that the nobody is becoming somebody," Shorty said. He peeled off a bill. "Here, get yourself new sneakers."

He shoved the money into Mark's hands and stomped down the steps. Finding that troublesome monkey was going to be harder than he thought.

Stopping Dodger from making messes was going to be harder than Eva thought. Just before dinner on Monday night, Eva worked on fitting Dodger into one of Jack's diapers. She measured, then cut out a hole for his tail.

Eva put the wriggling Dodger on his back and slid the clean diaper underneath his bottom. Thank goodness she had watched her mother diaper her brother hundreds of times. Eva knew what to do, but Dodger was no baby boy. He twisted, staring up at her with puzzled eyes. He tried to scoot away, but Eva held on

45

to him and wrapped the edges of the diaper securely around his furry waist.

"I can't have a litter box 'cause they'd see it, so we have no choice," she told a clearly unhappy Dodger. "Until you learn to use the potty."

And please let that be soon, Eva prayed. One more slip like this afternoon's, and the cat—no, the *monkey*—would really be out of the bag. Eva stared at Dodger, deep in thought, then stuck a little red doll's cap on his head. Adorable, she decided, only Dodger didn't agree.

The monkey shook his head from side to side and tried to pull the cap off.

"You don't like it?" She giggled.

He scooted out of sight under the bed in protest just as Tessa barged into the room. Eva jumped a mile.

"Dinner's ready," Tessa said. She wore a vampire shade of lipstick that matched her recently dyed hair and a bored expression on her face.

"It says Do Not Disturb on the door!" Eva said, glaring at Tessa. "Can't you at least knock? I'll be there in a sec."

"You'll be there *now*, Eva."

Casting a worried glance over her shoulder,

Eva marched out of the bedroom, making sure to close the door. This would be one meal she'd eat in a hurry. Anything to get back to Dodger as soon as possible.

She was practically inhaling her food when her mom dropped the first bomb.

"Eva, Mr. Flynn called to say you closed the elevator on his dog's nose and didn't let them in on purpose."

Eva remembered the incident clearly. Poor Dodger would have had a fit in the knapsack if that bulldog had gotten within two feet of them. But of course she couldn't tell her mother that. Her stepdad's sneezing across the table gave her a way out.

"I had to, Mom! If that dumb dog got hair all over me, just think how bad it might have been for Tom's allergy."

"As it is, I've been sneezing all afternoon," Tom complained, pulling out his handkerchief.

"See!" Eva said, pleased her little fib had worked.

She gulped down the last bit of food and immediately asked her mother for seconds. Dodger needed to be fed.

"Good girl!" Amy said, getting up with a pleased smile.

The phone rang, and Tom answered it.

"Eva, it's for you. Katie."

Finally! Someone she could tell about Dodger. Eva couldn't wait to share her secret with her best friend. She took the phone into the den for privacy.

"Can you keep a secret?" she whispered to Katie. "I mean, really swear to keep it? . . . No, I don't have a crush on anybody. This is a real secret, Katie!"

But before she could blurt out the news, the second and even bigger bomb dropped.

From across the room, something caught her eye. It was Dodger, waving hello to her from beside the living-room couch! He had escaped from the bedroom!

"Omigosh!" Eva said, wildly pulling at her hair. "I've got to go. I'll tell you tomorrow at school!"

She hung up, then began waving at Dodger. Shoo! Go back! Get out of here! For such an intelligent little guy, he simply wasn't getting it. Before Eva could rush over, Tom popped up between the den and the couch.

"What are you doing?" he asked, staring at her strange hand motions.

Eva put her arms down and smiled. She

hoped he couldn't tell how nervous she was. "Why, what's wrong?"

Curious, Tom turned around. There was nothing to see. Dodger had vanished.

"I need the phone, and your mom wants you back at the table," he said, sneezing as Eva walked over and handed him the phone.

Sitting once more at the dining-room table, Eva glanced nervously all around her. Where had Dodger gone? For sure he'd pop up right in front of her family, and then it was good-bye, Dodger.

Across from her, Jack leaned back in his high chair and pointed to the ceiling.

"Da! Da! Daaaadaaa!"

Eva looked up and saw Dodger moving across a wooden ceiling beam.

"Shut up, Jack!" she said in a deliberately rude voice. "Shut up and eat!"

Just as she had hoped, her mom turned her attention away from the baby to yell at *her*. By then Jack had started crying and forgotten all about the monkey. To calm him down, Amy grabbed a little doll and started chanting: "One little monkey, jumping on the bed. He fell off and bumped his head. Mama called—"

Eva collapsed in her chair from the strain. Was her mother trying to torture her? "Please! I hate all those rhymes!"

"Eva, what's the matter with you?" Amy said, puzzled. "Jack loves them."

From the corner of her eye, Eva spied Dodger sneaking back to the bedroom. She grabbed her plate and fork.

"I'm sorry, sing all you want," she said. "I'll go eat in my room for some peace and quiet. Excuse me from the table, please."

She rushed out, plate in hand. After tonight's weirdo performance, her family probably thought she had a few screws loose, but she didn't care. Right now she had more important things on her mind.

CHAPTER
7

Eva got up early Tuesday morning.

Now that she was taking care of Dodger, she had to be responsible for him as well as for herself. Somehow owning a pet made it easy to get up and clean her room. She put all her clothes away, made the bed, and had herself dressed in a neat and matching outfit by the time her mom came in.

"Good morning, Mom," Eva said.

Amy's jaw dropped.

"You cleaned up! You're dressed, you—"

Eva grinned at her. "I'm supposed to learn responsibility, remember? Let's have some breakfast—I'm starved!"

Eva ate a solid meal, sneaking seconds into her knapsack for Dodger. She made her own

51

lunch so she could take extra portions and left the apartment with plenty of time to go to school. This morning was special because she had Dodger with her. Eva made sure her friend Paul had gone on ahead so she could walk alone. With Dodger zipped up in her knapsack, Eva headed down the sidewalk with a confident step.

Back in the apartment, her mom couldn't get over the changes in her daughter.

"Something's up with Eva," Amy told her still-sleepy husband. "Last night she gave up her favorite show to do her homework. When I went to wake her up this morning, she was already washed and dressed. At breakfast she asked how Jack was doing on his toilet training. She was real curious about how I'm teaching him. Then she made her own lunch, with two bananas and an extra sandwich. . . ."

Tom sat up and shook his head. "Sounds like she met a guy. That would explain the two bananas and the extra sandwich."

"Right," Amy said. "And she's teaching this 'guy' to use the potty?"

* * *

Not realizing that her family was wondering about her, Eva was shooting down the spiral slide at the park. A scared Dodger hung on to her shoulders, his hands grabbing her face. Together the two of them hooted and screamed all the way down. They jumped on the swings and then played on the jungle gym. Her pet deserved some fun before she left him off for the day. Eva had worked it all out. There was no day care for monkeys in her neighborhood, but there was the pet shop. She'd ask Annie to keep Dodger for her while she was in school.

Eva put Dodger back into her knapsack and headed for the pet shop. She waited at a red light next to an elegant woman and several other people. The zipper of the knapsack silently opened. Eva didn't notice her monkey's hand creep out to steal a coin purse from the handbag of the well-dressed woman.

Eva slipped into the pet shop. She greeted Annie, then unzipped the knapsack. Dodger had fallen asleep.

"A capuchin!" Annie whispered. "Where did you get it?"

Eva stared at her. "Huh? Capu-what?"

"Isn't it a capuchin?" Annie asked.

Now Eva knew. Her pet was called a capuchin. Talk about special.

"I'm sure it is," Eva agreed quickly. "My, um, my father brought him from the Caribbean. He got it from a pirate. There's one thing he wasn't sure of: Is he going to grow up to be as big as a gorilla?"

Annie laughed. "Oh, no! I'd say he's probably fully grown now."

"Phew! I, ah, it's supposed to be like a surprise present for my mom, but my dad wants me to train him first. And since I know this place is safe because my mom would never, ever come in here—could you keep him while I'm at school?"

"Of course!" Annie said. "I'd love to."

Eva let out a big cheer. Now her major problem was solved.

"What a great surprise for your mom," Annie said with a smile. "Can you imagine her face when she sees it?"

Eva stopped cheering. That was the last thing she wanted to think about.

"No, and I don't really want to."

Eva left the pet shop and headed toward school.

She rounded the corner and saw Katie

waiting for her. But Katie wasn't alone—she had fifteen other girls with her.

"Eva! We've all been waiting to hear the news!" Katie said. "What happened?"

Eva glared at Katie and kept walking. All the girls followed, pressing in close to hear what Eva was saying.

"News?" she said. "It's not news, it's a secret!"

"We won't tell anybody!" the girls cried. "Promise!"

Katie shooed the girls away. "Go on, go inside! You can't listen to our secret!"

Grumbling, the group filed into the school building. Katie turned eagerly to Eva.

"Now you can tell me. What is it?" Katie asked. "I won't tell, I swear!"

Eva stopped and looked Katie straight in the eye.

"Katie, I can't. If I tell you, and you tell even one other person, it could ruin everything."

"Ruin what? Maybe I can help you," Katie promised. "I'm your best friend."

"Help me? I told you I had a secret and you told the whole class!"

Katie shot her a dark look. "You're not my friend anymore."

55

And without a backward glance, Katie ran inside.

Eva followed slowly, her lower lip trembling.

"Great best friend, Katie."

Shorty Kohn was hot on the monkey's trail. Shorty had only one goal: to get his monkey back. No monkey, no money. It was perfectly simple. Charlie and Drake were counting on him to pull off a big robbery, but he needed the monkey to do it.

Shorty had prepared a plan of attack. He had made a list of all the parks his monkey might have escaped to, and he had called the zoos. Pretending to be a doctor, Shorty had gotten on the phone and forced himself to sound polite and sincere.

"That's right, it's a very . . . ah . . . expensive brown capuchin trained to aid the quadriplegic. We assume the zoo would be the logical place to report a lost monkey, so I wanted to make sure yiz, ah, yous, ah . . . you, you knew where to reach me. Yeah, I'm Dr. Benjamin Stevenson, 555-1232. This is my beeper number, so please don't hesitate to call, day or night."

So far no one had called him back, but it

had been only a day. On Tuesday Shorty made the round of parks. He brought fliers he had made with a photo of the monkey above the words: "Monkey Missing. Big Reward. Call Dr. Benjamin Stevenson, 555-1232."

"Would you mind if I tacked these up around the park?" he asked a park attendant.

"Be my guest."

Shorty posted the fliers on bulletin boards in several parks. If the picture of the monkey and the magic words "Big Reward" didn't attract attention, nothing would. Feeling desperate, Shorty knew that without the monkey he could kiss his fifty grand goodbye. He *had* to find the monkey.

School was over, and Eva was feeling desperate, too. She shuffled out slowly to meet Tessa and Jack, her head hanging down. It had been a horrible day, one of the worst so far. Not only had she lost her best friend, but now Katie and Jesse were whispering about her, giggling as they walked past.

Eva felt a sympathetic hand on her shoulder.

"Rough day?" her teacher, Christine, asked.

Eva could only nod. Christine gave her a warm, understanding smile.

"I'll see you tomorrow, Eva."

That made Eva feel better. She smiled back and skipped ahead to join Tessa and the baby in a stroller. Her teenage cousin always had her nose in a magazine, so Eva figured she could dart in and out of the pet shop on the way home without Tessa noticing.

"Wait here a minute, okay?" Eva said when they reached the pet shop.

Sure enough, Tessa nodded and flipped the page of the fashion magazine she was reading. As soon as Eva entered the store, Annie opened Dodger's cage. He flew into Eva's arms and put a hand over her hat.

"He missed me!" she cried.

Suddenly the gloomy day became brighter. Eva might have lost Katie, but she had a true-blue friend in Dodger.

"He was a very big hit around here." Annie smiled. "All the customers fell in love with him." She paused as Eva packed Dodger into the knapsack. "The funniest thing is how he loves the cash register. I couldn't keep him away from it. He thinks it's the greatest toy in the world."

"Do you have any books about monkeys like this?" Eva asked.

"No, we don't. Try the library. You know, the one down the street?"

"Great idea!" Eva said. "See ya tomorrow!"

Hiding a grin, she ran out the door. She couldn't wait to lose Tessa and the baby and find out all she could about Dodger!

CHAPTER

8

She certainly owned a very special kind of pet, Eva realized later that afternoon. A helpful librarian had photocopied information on the capuchin monkey for her. Now Eva sat in her bedroom, studying the pages. Once in a while she glanced at Dodger. He seemed to be happy, playing with an old toy jewelry box on her bedroom shelf.

" 'Capuchins live in tropical forests,' " Eva read aloud. " 'They eat fruit, dry seeds, eggs, insects, spiders'—eeuuu!—'small animals such as lizards'—yuck!"

Eva turned to Dodger. Now he was fooling with her knapsack. "From now on I'm putting you on a low-yuck diet. No more lizards and no more spiders."

Eva returned to reading.

" 'At birth, capuchins depend on their mothers for food, protection, and transportation.' " Eva glanced proudly across the room at Dodger. So far she had been doing a good job as Dodger's mama.

" 'The females in the social group may mate with different males,' " she continued reading. " 'Members may leave and new members join in.' "

At that, Eva looked up at two family photos on the wall. One showed Amy, Peter, and Eva when she was younger. The other showed Amy, Tom, Eva, and Jack.

"We're not different at all!" she announced happily to Dodger.

She watched her pet scamper onto the bed, then leap from bedpost to bedpost. It looked like it was a game to him, but it was making her dizzy!

" 'Like all New World monkeys,' " Eva continued, " 'capuchins are at home in areas rich with trees. They spend most of their time up in the branches.' "

Eva stared over at her flying pet and smiled. No wonder he liked swinging around her bedposts. Tomorrow she'd make sure to take

61

Dodger into the park so he could play in some real trees. She went back to the book.

"'Monkeys can use their tail to grasp branches, swing, and climb. Their feet are larger and more powerful than their hands.'"

Dodger was now hanging by his tail from the top of the bedpost, gripping Eva's stuffed monkey in his foot. Eva burst into laughter, but Dodger suddenly dropped the toy and scooted under the bed. A moment later the door opened and Jack toddled in. Instead of yelling at him to leave, Eva allowed her brother to stay. She shut the door behind him, then peered under the bed.

"He's okay," she called softly to Dodger. "He won't rat on us. He can't talk."

She turned to Jack. "Want to meet somebody? Wait."

Eva commanded Dodger to come out. He slid out nervously. An excited Jack pointed, babbled, and charged at the monkey, who leapt into Eva's arms for protection.

"Don't worry," she reassured a trembling Dodger. "This is my brother, Jack. Jack, this is Dodger."

Eva set Dodger down in front of Jack, who let out a big giggle. Eva laughed along with him. Dodger squatted in front of them and covered his ears.

"Isn't he cute?" Eva asked Jack. "See, he's wearing diapers like you. You guys play while I finish reading."

Eva returned to her desk but sneaked glances over her shoulder at Jack and Dodger. She was bursting to share her secret. Jack was perfect—he couldn't tell anyone! Eva grinned as Dodger curled his strong tail around Jack's ankle and yanked. Jack fell down on his diapered butt but got up smiling. He reached for Dodger.

Both "babies" were getting into it.

Eva couldn't have been more pleased.

Over the next few weeks Eva was glad she had introduced her monkey to Jack. The three of them kept the secret from Amy and Tom, although Tom still sneezed and wondered if he were suffering from a cold. Together Eva, Jack, and Dodger snuck out in the afternoons, to play in the park, have a ball in the pet store, and try to give Dodger a much-needed bath. If someone had told Eva a month before that she'd be having so much fun with her brother, she would have laughed in his face. But Jack wasn't such a bad little kid. In fact, he wasn't the little monster she had always thought. She changed the sign on her bedroom door from No Jack Allowed to Only Jack Allowed.

Eva's mom passed by and did a double take.

"Tom! Come here, come see this!"

Tom joined Amy and read Eva's corrected sign. Amy was so touched, she nearly cried. And Tom was impressed as he tried to stifle a sneeze.

"Boy! What have we done right?" Tom said.

"This is major," Amy whispered happily. "Major . . ."

Things were going so well something bad had to happen. And sure enough, the very next morning it did. The Gregory family was finishing breakfast at the dining-room table. Eva had her oatmeal, Amy was reading the paper, and a sneezing Tom kept dialing a number from the yellow pages when he wasn't feeding Jack. Eva figured the line was busy because Tom punched in the number over and over.

"Oh, I meant to ask you," he said to Eva. "This guy that you're going out with—"

Eva and Amy looked at each other.

"I mean your boyfriend," Tom said, correcting himself. "Excuse me, this little pal at school, who you always make the extra lunch for . . ."

Eva stared down at her bowl of oatmeal, her heart beating faster.

"Does he have a dog?" Tom finished, then sneezed.

Eva gulped. "I don't know who you're talking about," she said.

She quickly gathered her bowl and was preparing to leave the table when Tom's call finally went through.

"Hello, is this Pest Terminator?" Tom said.

This was it. This was the moment she had been dreading. Without thinking, Eva jumped up and pressed the disconnect lever on the phone, cutting Tom off.

She stared at Tom in horror. "Why are you calling a pet terminator?"

"Pest Terminator, Eva, *pest*," her stepdad corrected her. "I haven't stopped sneezing in weeks. We must have rats."

Eva laughed with relief. "Rats, exactly! I meant to tell you—I'm sure I saw one, or heard one, in the walls or the ceilings. I definitely think we have rats."

Eva thought about rats throughout the day. She thought about the men who would come to kill the rats. What if they came to the

65

apartment and figured out that the Gregory family had a *monkey*, not a rat, problem? It was too scary to think about!

As soon as school was over, Eva hurried out to meet Tessa.

"Did you see the rat guys?" Eva asked as Tessa pushed the stroller.

Tessa barely looked up from her magazine. "Huh? Rat Guys? Must be a new band, because I never heard of them."

"Can they tell if it's not rats?"

Tessa mumbled something, then began chattering about a rock star's car.

"Listen to me!" Eva cried. "Do these guys work on weekends? They can't, right?"

That got Tessa's attention. "You're right, I can't work this weekend. I'm going to *four* concerts, and you're going to your dad's."

Eva stopped dead. "Omigosh! My dad! One on one for two whole days!"

She had completely forgotten about this date. She adored her father and loved visiting Venice Beach, but what about Dodger? Who would take care of her pet?

Annie . . . Eva's face brightened. Annie would look after Dodger for her. Then she remembered that she had lied to Annie in the beginning. She had told Annie that Dodger was a surprise present for her mom and had to be kept hidden from her during the day. Now the lie would backfire.

When Eva raced into the pet shop, Dodger immediately jumped up in his cage by the wall and made welcoming noises. But Eva had to talk to Annie first.

"Annie, I . . . I have to go to my dad's this weekend, and . . ."

"How great!" Annie beamed at her. "You won't have to worry about hiding Dodger, right?"

"Right," Eva said in a small voice.

Wrong, Eva thought in despair. Annie opened the cage, and Dodger happily jumped into Eva's knapsack. Eva zipped up the sack and rejoined Tessa and Jack outside the shop.

"Want to go to the park?" Tessa suggested as they headed down the street.

The park? How could Eva enjoy the park when the worst problem in the world was dangling over her head?

CHAPTER

9

Two hours later Eva still hadn't come up with a solution to the world's biggest problem.

What was she going to do about Dodger that weekend?

She lay on the floor of her bedroom, facedown, and banged her head over and over against the rug. It didn't really hurt, and she usually got her best ideas this way.

Right across from her Dodger was stretched out, imitating her weird head-banging act.

"Where am I going to hide him?" Eva chanted. "How can I leave him here? What should I tell Dad? How can I change this? Who can I give him to?"

After each question she banged her head and Dodger did the same.

Tessa interrupted her. "Eva! Your father's on the phone!" she called.

At the sound of her voice, Dodger scampered into the bathroom. Maybe hiding wasn't such a bad idea, Eva thought. She ducked behind the bed.

But Tessa wasn't going away. "Eva!" she bellowed. "Did you hear me?"

There was no way out. Eva was trapped, and she knew it. Slowly she got to her feet. Tears glistened in her eyes.

"I'm coming!" Eva shouted.

She stood in the middle of the room, wiping her eyes.

"I have to stay calm," she whispered to herself.

Just then Dodger ran out of the bathroom with a piece of toilet paper in his hand. He hopped into her arms and dabbed at the tears with the toilet tissue. Touched, Eva looked at him.

"Thanks, pal. I'll be okay."

She didn't really believe it, though. She'd *never* be okay if they took Dodger away from her. Wait a sec, that gave her an idea!

"Hey, maybe I shouldn't be okay. I'm sick! Toxic! Temperature of 104!"

Making a weird face and clutching dramatically at her stomach, she staggered out of the room and picked up the extension in her mom's bedroom.

"Hello, Dad?" she got out with a croak.

"Honey, what's wrong?" Peter said. "You sound awful."

"I *feel* awful."

"Well then, maybe I don't have such bad news after all."

Eva frowned. "Bad news? What bad news?"

"I was calling to say I can't see you this weekend."

The false temperature and phony illness disappeared immediately. So did Eva's problem. Her droopy face perked up, and she danced a little jig in celebration.

"They switched my flight schedule just a few hours ago," her father explained. "I'm already at the airport. I have to be in Vancouver until Monday. Anyway, if you're so sick—"

"I'm feeling better, thanks," Eva said in a normal voice.

Much, *much* better, she thought with a huge grin.

"Sweetheart, I'll make it up to you, I mean it."

"Don't be upset, Dad. I love you!" Eva cried.

"I love you, too. Now hang up and let me leave a message for your mom."

Eva hung up but stayed beside the phone, thinking. The phone rang again. The machine picked up. As Peter left a message, a light bulb the size of Dodger popped on over Eva's head. An idea as brilliant as a thousand watts suddenly came to her. How clever, how smart, how *awesome* she was! And if she could pull it off, she and Dodger would have the best weekend ever!

She came back to earth when the machine beeped and the electronic voice announced, "Thursday. Five fifteen P.M."

Eva glanced down and pressed a button on the machine.

"I will erase your messages," the electronic voice stated.

Eva grinned—part one of the plan was working—then picked up the receiver and dialed again. Time to work on part two.

"Hello?" her one-time best friend in the entire world answered.

"Katie, it's me," Eva said.

71

"I'm not speaking to you," Katie said in a cold voice.

"Who cares?" Eva said. "I need to talk to your mother."

Katie was confused, but went to call her mother. Let her be confused, Eva thought with a little grin. Katie would know soon enough what the plan was, and then they'd both share a good laugh. When Katie's mom came on, Eva went into her carefully thought-out speech.

Later that night Eva gave another speech, this time to her own mom. She didn't like lying to her mother, but sometimes she just had to. Especially when Dodger was concerned.

Amy, Tessa, and Eva were sitting at the dining-room table, finishing dinner.

Amy glanced across at Eva. "What's the scoop for the weekend?"

"I'm going to Dad's," Eva said.

"Tessa told me he called, but I didn't find a message," Amy said.

Careful now, Eva thought. This was the tricky part. She kept her voice normal.

"I handled everything," Eva said. Boy, had she ever! "He said he'll be waiting for me. And, Mom? Katie said they're going to the beach, so they could drop me off if you want."

72

Amy and Tessa exchanged glances. Eva could tell they were impressed. She really had her act together these days.

"I'll call Missie after dinner," Amy said, getting up to clear the table.

Eva popped up to help her mom.

Tessa ruffled Eva's hair. "You're a cool little babe, you know that?"

A lot cooler than you realize, Eva thought with a private smile. This weekend was going to be something else!

It was time to tell Katie the secret.

Eva and Katie were sitting in the back of the station wagon on Saturday, being driven by Katie's mom to Venice Beach. The knapsack containing Dodger rested by Eva's duffel bag. For most of the ride Katie sat turned away from Eva, pretending Eva was invisible. Eva kept glancing over at her, wondering when to show her the surprise. She could usually tell Katie anything, but today Katie was giving her the silent treatment. Even Katie's mom had noticed.

"What's the matter with you guys? You're so quiet."

"Maybe we don't have anything to say to each other," Katie said in an icicle voice.

Eva decided this was the moment to let

Katie in on the secret. She grabbed a scrap of paper and a crayon off the messy car floor and scribbled: "Do you swear?"

Katie read the note with an excited smile. She crossed her fingers over her sealed lips and stuck the wadded-up note in her mouth.

That was good enough for Eva. She nodded toward the back. The girls slipped off their seat belts and slid over the backseat.

"Are you ready?" Eva whispered in Katie's ear. "Don't scream."

Katie nodded solemnly. Eva unzipped the knapsack. A bright-eyed Dodger peered up at them. Katie spit the wad of paper clear to the front seat, then covered her mouth to stifle a scream. The two girls burst into squealing giggles.

Katie's mom didn't take her eyes off the road. "That's better," she said. "Now go back to your seats and put on your seat belts."

Eva stared out the window at the familiar sights and street signs as they got closer. She knew it wouldn't take long to reach her father's condo. Would everything really go as planned? Her heart thumped a little faster as the station wagon pulled up in front of the modern two-story house surrounded by trees and plants.

74

Eva craned her neck and was relieved to see her dad's Jeep parked in the open garage. Now Katie's mother would think her father was home.

Eva quickly hopped out with her knapsack and duffel bag and pointed to the Jeep. "He's here, see? Must be waiting for me in the backyard."

"Just do me a favor, Eva," Katie's mom said. "Make sure he's there and then come out and give us a wave."

"Okee-dokee!" Eva shouted as she disappeared behind the house. She reappeared seconds later, giving them a thumbs-up sign and a cheery wave.

"Thanks for the ride!" she called.

Now please go, she begged privately. She got her wish when the station wagon pulled away, Katie waving to her from the backseat.

"Perfect," she said, eyeballing the house.

She hurried to the front door but was surprised to find it locked. Her smile faded.

"Except I don't have a key," she groaned. "Dodger, we're in trouble."

She unzipped the knapsack, and Dodger jumped out.

"Two whole days alone, free to play and do anything we want—and I blew it!"

CHAPTER

10

Dodger jumped into action.

He grabbed a crumpled bag from Eva's knapsack and began climbing a tree. He reached the top quickly and jumped onto the second-story ledge of the house. Eva watched in amazement as he wrestled with a locked window.

"He's totally trying to get us in!"

Dodger moved to a small, round attic window. Eva couldn't quite see what he did, but she cheered as Dodger nimbly jumped inside. She hurried onto the porch and pressed an ear to the front door. Would the little guy know he had to come and open the door for her?

"Dodger! Open up!" Eva shouted.

The sound of footsteps on the sidewalk made her spin around. A neighbor was staring at her.

"Dad?" she called, to cover for the slip. She grinned in embarrassment at the neighbor. "My dad locked me out by mistake," she explained.

The man gave an understanding nod and turned away.

Seconds went by, then minutes. What was Dodger doing in there? Eva pressed her face against the window and peered inside. No sign of her pet.

"Open the door!" she shouted.

Incredibly, the lock clicked. The door opened. There stood Dodger in his diapers, looking amazingly proud of himself. Eva raised her hand. So did Dodger. Just as she had taught him, they slapped a high five.

"You're unreal!" she exclaimed with a huge grin.

Eva switched the lock on the door handle so that it opened from the outside. Can't afford any more goof-ups, she thought. But just as she walked into the living room, an ear-splitting, heart-stopping shriek shattered the silence. Eva shrieked back and dropped her bags.

"I forgot the alarm!" Eva shouted above the whooping sound.

Terrified, Dodger leapt onto her shoulders and began whooping along with the alarm. He wrapped his trembling arms around her face.

Eva couldn't see, couldn't hear, couldn't think. She felt like a spin drier gone out of control. She raced back out, to a panel on the wall. The little red lights were blinking furiously. Dodger was twisting on her shoulders, completely covering her eyes.

"Let go, I can't see!" Eva said, pulling a furry arm away.

She stared at the panel in horror. "He punches numbers, but which ones? Why don't I ever pay attention to the important things in life?"

She started hitting buttons, any buttons. Nothing happened. Feeling desperate, Eva muttered, "Here goes," and slapped the entire control panel. Silence. The shrieking stopped.

"Phew." Eva sighed and collapsed against the wall. Talk about nerve-shattering experiences.

But the ordeal wasn't over. As soon as the

alarm had stopped, the phone started ringing. Eva grabbed Dodger and froze. They both turned to stare at the phone and answering machine in the living room.

The machine clicked on. "This is Ned at West Tec Security. If you're there, Mr. Boylan, please pick up."

Eva dived for the phone. "Hello? Yeah, we're here. Uh huh, everything's fine." She made a face at Dodger. "See, my dad had to go to the bathroom when we came in, and he forgot to shut off the alarm." She paused, listening, then laughed. "When you gotta go, you gotta go. Yes, I'll tell him. Thanks for checking, it's all A-OK!"

She hung up the phone and slid to the floor in an exhausted heap.

"This is not as easy as I thought."

It got worse.

Dodger suddenly began acting like her baby brother in his I-want-to-touch-everything mood. The monkey darted around the living room, picking up silver picture frames. Eva ran over and pulled them out of his hands.

"Don't touch those things! If we break something, my dad will know somebody was here. Come on, I'm starved!"

79

They headed for the kitchen. More bad news: The refrigerator was completely empty, except for some eggs, a jug of water, and a jar of mustard. Eva slammed the refrigerator door with a groan.

"Dad didn't go shopping because he wasn't going to be here," she said. "And I didn't bring any money because I'm stupid. Stupid, stupid."

She looked down at Dodger with scared eyes. Dodger immediately hugged her knees and copied her scared expression. This wouldn't do, Eva thought. She had to take care of her pet. And that meant making some money if the weekend was going to work.

Eva knew that the best place to panhandle for money was at nearby Venice Beach. Eva snapped her fingers and carried Dodger into the garage. She pulled her bike out and mounted an old baby seat on the back.

"Everybody on the boardwalk does it," Eva said, trying to reassure herself as well as Dodger. "If you don't have money, and you can't find it, you've got to make it."

Dodger was shifting from one foot to the other and shooting nervous looks at the bike. One hand kept picking at his little red hat.

Eva picked him up with a soothing smile.

He really was her baby! She carefully strapped Dodger into the rear seat and then hopped on the bike.

"Have you ever been on a bike before?" she asked as she wheeled out of the garage. "It's fun. Ready, Freddie? Let's go make money!"

Shorty had lain low for the last few weeks, sticking close to his trailer. The search for his monkey had fizzled out, and without the monkey he couldn't work the boardwalk. Plus Charlie and Drake would be hot on his trail. If they found him, it would mean trouble. But Shorty could stay holed up in his ratty trailer for only so long. He had to get out, and when he did he headed for the boardwalk.

He walked along now in the warm sunshine, taking in the action and checking out the tourists. Who knew? Maybe, just maybe, his monkey would turn up.

Eva pedaled slowly along the bike path that ran alongside the boardwalk. She could hear Dodger chattering nervously in the baby seat. He was making funny little hooting noises.

"Boy, are you excited!" Eva said with a laugh. "I knew you'd love it!"

Dodger *hated* it.

This was where he and Shorty always worked the crowd, and Shorty could be here, right now, waiting to grab him. Dodger glanced over his shoulder and immediately shut up. There was Shorty in regular clothes and a straw hat, coming up the boardwalk behind them. Dodger frantically slid inside Eva's open knapsack.

But Eva skidded to a halt and moved the bike out of the bike path.

"No, Dodger, no," she said, reaching in and pulling him out. "Down here you don't have to hide. Hey, you're going to be the special attraction today."

She zipped the knapsack shut. Dodger peeked around and hooted. Shorty was getting closer! Dodger dived for cover under Eva's baggy shirt. Eva laughed and chased the monkey back out into the light—just as Shorty strolled past them.

Eva plopped a trembling Dodger back into the baby seat. He peeked over Eva's shoulder. Had they lost Shorty in the crowd? No, he was right up ahead! In a total panic, Dodger hopped down and tried to turn the front wheel of the bike in the opposite direction. But Eva didn't understand.

"Sorry, we can't go home yet," she said, picking him up and putting him back in his seat. "We have to find the right spot and try to earn some money."

Dodger was desperate. Shorty was coming closer. Any minute Shorty would turn and see him. Dodger tugged the pad off the back of his seat and propped it up in front of his face. But then Eva veered off the bike path and began riding on the boardwalk. Now Shorty was in plain view! The pad was on the wrong side, and Dodger was completely exposed.

There was only one thing to do. Dodger jumped off the bike and scampered over to a pile of cardboard boxes and trash cans in front of a seedy-looking restaurant. Now he was on his own.

Shorty had stopped at a nearby phone stand to make a call. Dodger jumped headfirst into one of the large cardboard boxes. Using the box for cover, Dodger stumbled across the boardwalk. He blindly bumped into hairy knees, skateboards, and baby strollers. He was going to get away, until a barking dog tipped the box over. Exposed and terrified, Dodger took cover behind a tree. Turning, he spotted Shorty moving closer. Dodger ran behind a crowd of people. Unfortunately, those people were watching a snake charmer. Dodger scooted through all the legs in the crowd—and came face-to-face with a ten-foot boa! He screeched.

Not more than fifteen feet away, Shorty heard the screech. His monkey was here! Shorty plowed through the crowd around the snake charmer and spotted the monkey.

The chase was on.

Dodger scurried under a fruit stand in the market. A customer screamed and stumbled backward, pulling boxes over. Oranges and apples tumbled to the ground. Tourists and in-line skaters hit the fruit and went flying.

Shorty heard the yelling. All the commotion could mean only one thing: His monkey was in the middle of that mess. He called for his monkey and ran, crashing into tables. Tie-dyed T-shirts, hand-carved animals, and colorful toys all shot up in the air like giant confetti. The merchants screamed at him.

Dodger seized his opportunity. He darted under the stands to a nearby popcorn wagon, then took off across the playground. Reaching the bike path, he hopped a ride on the roof of a baby carrier attached to a mom's bicycle.

Shorty snarled and pushed a man off his skateboard. No way would he let his monkey escape. Wheeling away, Shorty tried to catch up to the monkey, but it was no good. He fell off the stolen skateboard, then scrambled to his feet and took a shortcut across the grass.

In another few seconds he'd reach the monkey.

Dodger jumped off the baby carrier and headed for the beach. A girl with a huge kite was letting the string out, waiting for the breeze to kick up. What a great place to hide!

Dodger scrambled underneath the kite for protection. The girl spotted Dodger and screamed. Dodger leapt onto the crossbar just as she dropped the strings. It was too late to jump off!

A strong breeze suddenly lifted the kite off the ground. Dodger gripped the crossbar with all his strength as he went flying high into the air. The kite dipped and twirled and streaked through the sky.

Below, Shorty stared up at the sight. Hurriedly he wrestled the strings away from the boy who now controlled the kite. If he could somehow bring the monkey down . . .

A tap on his shoulder ended that plan. A hulking lifeguard stood behind him with the kite's rightful owner. Shorty knew he was no match for those muscles.

Besides, the kite was gliding down toward the bike path. The monkey would be landing —or crashing—any minute.

Shorty couldn't believe what he saw next. His monkey jumped from the crossbars of the kite right into the baby seat on a girl's bike. Talk about luck! Cursing under his breath, Shorty took off.

Her idea had been brilliant, Eva thought as she slowly pedaled along. The boardwalk was crowded with tourists, and that meant better chances to make some money. Now, where to pull off to do their act? Eva checked the boardwalk carefully, trying to find the perfect spot for her and Dodger.

She was skirting a group of older bikers when she suddenly felt a thump in the baby carrier. Eva grinned. Dodger had been awfully quiet back there, but now he must be getting restless. Looking over her shoulder, she said, "Careful, or you'll fall down!"

Dodger just stared at her with a funny expression on his face.

Keeping the girl and the monkey in sight, Shorty chased after them. Another few minutes and the monkey would be his. But suddenly, out of nowhere, Charlie and Drake popped up, blocking his path. They didn't look happy.

"Where have you been?" Drake growled. "You were supposed to check in, tell us how the training's going."

Of all the rotten timing! Shorty craned his neck, getting a good look at Eva as she pedaled toward the boardwalk.

"Does it have to be now?" he said. "Training's great—I'm trying to get in shape myself, jogging, see?"

Shorty took a running step past the men, but Charlie clamped a hand around his throat. The two goons meant business, all right. Shorty swallowed hard.

"I got the boss breathing down my neck about this monkey thing now," Drake said in a menacing voice. "My job is on the line. I need to know I can depend on you."

"I'm sorry," Shorty mumbled. "I didn't want ya to worry. The monkey gets a cold,

87

nothing serious. We was training at the vet's. It's all under control."

Shorty gave the men his most convincing, sincere smile. Would they buy his story?

Drake and Charlie bought it. Charlie released his hand from Shorty's throat.

"C'mon. Let's take a walk," Charlie said, grabbing Shorty by one elbow. Drake took the other, and they escorted him to their limo.

"Yeah," Drake said. "And then we'll take a little ride."

Mumbling under his breath, Shorty made a vow: Before the weekend was over, he'd track down that girl on the bike and get his monkey back.

CHAPTER

11

Eva couldn't do it.

Not in a hundred, not in a thousand, not in a million years.

She simply could not bring herself to beg for money. She had parked the bicycle, then carried Dodger toward the most crowded part of the boardwalk. It all looked so easy when other people did it, but when she stuck her hand out to ask for money, her fingers curled up in embarrassment.

"Dodger, I—I can't do it," she said in a small voice.

Dodger went to work. He climbed down from her arms and sprang into action. He tipped his hat, he bowed from the waist, he jumped into people's arms. He collected quite a bit of money for his lovable antics.

This monkey had talent! Eva thought, amazed by the size of the crowds he attracted. And if her pet could work so hard, then she could do her bit, as well.

"Step right up," she said loudly, "and pet this rare and beautiful monkey! He's sweet, he's neat, give yourself a treat! Don't be shy, give it a try! Come one, come all, ladies and gentlemen, boys and girls!"

A young Japanese couple with a camcorder and a regular camera drew close to Eva and Dodger. Dodger tipped his hat and bowed, then climbed into the man's arms. The delighted woman offered her camera to Eva.

Eva waved it away. "No, thanks, I don't take cameras—cash only. Understand? Money."

"You take picture, please?" the Japanese woman said.

"Oh, sure!" What a dumb mistake.

Eva took a shot of the couple with Dodger perched between them. When she handed back the camera, the woman handed her a dollar. A whole dollar! Eva's jaw dropped.

And the money piled in. An hour later Eva and Dodger were still at it, and Eva's cap jingled with change and some bills. If this kept up, they wouldn't have to worry about a thing for the rest of the weekend. This was becoming a lot of fun. Eva raised her voice and really got into it: "Step right up and see the wonderful Caribbean pirate monkey! Pet him for a quarter, pictures for a buck, rub his head and get good luck!"

Suddenly a man in the crowd yelled, "My wallet's gone! Somebody stole my wallet!"

Eva's face fell as Dodger jumped straight into her arms. Of all the times for something like this to happen, right when she and Dodger were getting the hang of it.

Everyone turned to look at the man who had shouted.

"There's a pickpocket in the crowd!" he insisted.

People began searching their pockets and checking their purses.

"My earrings!" someone cried.

"My bracelet!" said another.

Within seconds the crowd had melted away. The party was over. Still carrying Dodger, Eva walked back to her bike, then sank onto a nearby bench. She jingled her cap, which was loaded with money.

"It's okay, we got enough," she whispered to Dodger. "You're brilliant, you know that? We made a fortune!"

Eva began counting the money with raised eyebrows. It was even more than she had hoped to make—nearly ten dollars in quarters and several single dollar bills. Then Dodger opened his furry paw to drop another bill in her cap. Eva's jaw dropped.

"Whoa! Who gave you twenty bucks? They must have made a mistake!" She giggled and snapped the twenty. "But that's not our fault, is it? Dodger, this is our lucky day! Let's go to the store and stock up on food," Eva said, jumping up. "I'm starved!"

She strapped Dodger back on the bike and rode to the nearby supermarket, praising her pet the entire way. After parking the bike outside, she carefully zipped Dodger into the knapsack and entered the store. She walked up and down the aisles, putting orange juice, milk, syrup, and a box of cereal in her shopping cart. The knapsack, now only half zipped, was twitching. Dodger was getting restless.

"Stop it," Eva whispered. "They know my dad here."

She brought the cart up front, where a

bored young cashier began to ring up the items.

"Cash, check, or credit card?" he asked.

"Huh? Just regular money," Eva said.

As she handed him the twenty-dollar bill, Eva noticed an older woman cashier at the next register staring at her. Thinking Dodger might be acting up, Eva shifted the knapsack around. She got her grocery bag and change and hurried to the exit.

But the woman cashier suddenly stepped into her path.

"Little girl, can I look into your backpack?"

That's all she needed. "No, why?" Eva said.

Now the other customers were staring. Eva began to squirm.

The woman cashier whispered to the guy who had rung up her items: "I know her dad. He has a charge account here." Then she faced Eva directly. "I just want to see what you've got in there."

"It's personal," Eva said.

"Where's your dad?" the woman asked.

"He's at the stores across the street," Eva said, thinking quickly. "Can I please go now?"

Eva took a step toward the door, but then she saw more trouble coming—the store manager.

"What's going on?" the man asked.

"I think this little girl has been shoplifting," the woman announced.

Eva's jaw dropped. "I didn't steal anything!"

"Then why don't you want me to look in your sack?" the woman challenged.

She had a point, Eva thought. The bulging knapsack probably did look suspicious. But to think she'd shoplift! This was a bad situation, sure to get worse, and it made her nervous and scared.

As if sensing this, the store manager took her aside and knelt to be on eye level with her. He put a reassuring hand on her shoulder.

"Look, hon, we all make mistakes. All I want you to do is walk up an aisle, and if there's anything in your backpack you forgot to pay for, just leave it there. If you do, I'll forget the whole thing."

Not knowing what else to do, Eva followed his orders. Shoulders tense, totally embarrassed, she walked down an aisle until she was out of everyone's sight and then stopped. Hurriedly she set the knapsack down. Unzipping it, she whispered, "Dodger, I have to leave you somewhere, then I'll—"

She broke off, shocked at what she saw. There was Dodger, dipping a stolen chicken drumette into a stolen jar of peanut butter and taking a carefree bite.

Her pet was a thief! Dodger had shoplifted these items behind her back, and now the store manager and the suspicious woman were staring at her from the end of the aisle. Her mouth open in shock, and feeling as if a ten-pound basketball had just smacked her in the stomach, Eva snatched the chicken and peanut butter out of Dodger's hands and zipped up the knapsack. She placed the stolen items back on the shelf. Wishing that the floor would open up and swallow her, she returned to the front of the store. Everyone was staring at her—customers, cashiers, the kind-faced store manager. In tight-lipped silence she grabbed the groceries she'd paid for and stormed out of the store.

"How could you do this to me?" she cried as she ran to her bike. "You made me a thief!"

Eva was in for another shock when she got back to the condo. She was scolding Dodger, trying to make him understand how wrong stealing was.

"Why did you have to do that?" she demanded, pacing the living room. "If they caught you, I'd have to get rid of you! Is that what you want?"

Dodger sat on the coffee table, hanging his head. Then he looked up and blew her a kiss.

Eva stopped pacing. "Don't you kiss up to me now! You have no idea what you did, do you?"

Dodger jumped off the table. He dragged the knapsack over to Eva and began fishing inside.

"Yeah, you should hide in there and think about what a bad little monkey you've been!" Eva told him.

But instead of hiding, Dodger pulled out a gold watch and dangled it in front of her.

Eva's eyes widened. "What is that? Where did you get it?"

When she snatched it out of Dodger's hands, he dug into the sack and pulled out a man's wallet.

"You ripped off this stuff, too?" she shrieked.

With a sick feeling in her stomach, Eva overturned the knapsack. A dazzling collection of rings, earrings, bracelets, and money poured out onto the coffee table.

Dodger sat back with a huge grin on his face. Eva dropped onto the sofa and buried her face in her hands.

"Oh, no!" she whispered. "This stuff is from

those people on the beach! This is horrible, *horrible!*"

Shorty was feeling pretty horrible as well.

He shuffled along the Venice boardwalk at twilight, mumbling to himself. This had been a rotten day, from start to finish. He had found his monkey, then lost him, and the little girl could be anywhere by now.

Then the two goons had taken him for a little ride to a big mansion. "The monkey will drop in here to do some shopping," Drake had growled at him. Shorty had swallowed. He knew that shopping meant stealing. But could he find his monkey in time? Drake and Charlie had their own doubts. They'd slapped an electronic surveillance bracelet—a tracking device—on his ankle.

"This is just to make sure we know where you are," Charlie had said in a warning voice before they'd ditched him at the trailer.

Shorty dropped onto a bench with a groan. Without the monkey, he was dead. And come Monday, the two goons would track him down. And when they did . . .

He whacked at the surveillance anklet in fury, then howled in pain. There had to be some way out! He glanced around the nearly deserted boardwalk. Madame Tisa, a tarot card reader, was sitting at a table close by. Desperate, Shorty plopped down in front of her.

"Tisa, look into my cards," he pleaded.

The woman solemnly stared down at the cards.

"I see trouble. Woman trouble," she began. "She left and took with her a boy."

Shorty cut Tisa off. "Yeah, yeah. Who cares about that? What else?"

Tisa continued. "I see men. Dangerous men. Men who want to hurt you."

Shorty blinked at her. "They want to hurt me?"

"They are capable of great violence."

"That's why I need to find my monkey!"

Tisa looked up. "A monkey? A brown-and-black one?"

"That's it! You see him?"

"I *really* saw him." Tisa nodded. "This afternoon, heading toward Lincoln on the back of a little girl's bike."

A lead! Shorty jumped up in excitement. Maybe he was closer to the monkey than he thought!

CHAPTER

12

Eva sat on the sofa in a daze. She stared into space, remembering all the tricks and stunts Dodger had pulled.

"He's a break-in artist too," she groaned. "He knew exactly how to get into this house!"

Oh boy, what else could he do? Eva had to find out. She'd test him. She walked into the kitchen and found Dodger eating by the refrigerator.

"Hide!" Eva suddenly shouted.

Dodger immediately scampered behind the refrigerator.

"Police!" Eva cried.

Dodger darted out of the kitchen.

"That's the kind of English you understand," Eva said in a disgusted voice. "You're not from the circus, you're from a gang!"

She stood there, thinking. What was she going to do? She couldn't lose Dodger, she simply couldn't.

In bed that night she came up with the answer to her problem.

"I bet you don't even know what 'stealing' means," Eva said. Dodger lay beside her, stroking her hair in typical monkey fashion. "The books never said anything about you being a thief." She began patting the monkey's head.

"You do it because somebody trained you. Whoever it was, I hate them! I'm going to *un*-train you. Starting tomorrow, I will *dis*-teach you to *un*-learn every single thing those jerks taught you!"

Early the next morning, Eva took Dodger out to the backyard for his first "un-training" session. She had set up a table with money, jewelry, and pickpocket-type objects, as well as bananas and strawberries and some small toys.

Dodger went straight for a dollar bill.

Eva stuck her face in the monkey's and shook her head. "No, Dodger! No good! No!"

She placed Dodger's hand on a piece of fruit, then smiled and petted him. Dodger seemed to enjoy this, but then he hooked his tail around a bracelet. Eva slapped the tail and removed the bracelet. Dodger grabbed it back and slapped Eva's hand.

"This isn't going to be easy." Eva sighed.

She pointed once more at the goody-laden table. Dodger eyed a bright red ball but palmed an earring instead. When Eva wanted him to choose between a strawberry and a bracelet, he reached for both. Eva shook her head. This was more work than she'd bargained for.

Shorty was working, too. Up and down the neighborhood he talked to people, showed them pictures of the monkey, described the little girl. His leads were narrowing. He was getting close. Some kids on skateboards directed him to a local supermarket. Now he was glad he had hooked the trailer to his truck. If he found the monkey he could take off fast and not worry about anyone following him home.

Shorty hummed under his breath as he parked by the supermarket. He had a good feeling about this. He got an even better feeling after talking to a woman cashier who remembered the little girl all too well.

"A cute little kid like that," Shorty said to the cashier, shaking his head. "Can you imagine? She stole from me, totally ripped me off."

"I'm not surprised." The woman sniffed. "I caught her in here yesterday trying to shoplift." She leaned forward, lowering her voice. "My boss let her go. Didn't even tell her dad."

Shorty frowned. "If I knew where she lived, I'd go talk to her old man right now."

The cashier glanced toward the office, making sure the manager wasn't around. She led Shorty to a computer terminal.

"I know him, he's single—I mean, divorced," she whispered. "He's got a charge account here. I'll give you the address."

Eva was talking on the phone in the condo's living room. She had the yellow pages open on the coffee table, along with the money and valuables Dodger had stolen.

"The address is 227 Hillcrest," Eva said into the receiver. "Hold on." Turning her head away, she bellowed, "Daaad! Are you still in the shower?" She spoke into the receiver again. "Sorry, he can't pick up. He said just send the cab over. Thanks!"

She hung up, then gathered all the bills into a wad. Dodger stared at her, obviously puzzled.

Eva scowled at him. "What are you staring at? I'm innocent, you're the one who did it. I'm just using it to get us safely home."

She jammed the wad of bills into her knapsack. She wished she could jam the last two days inside as well. Dodger had been such a perfect pet before she discovered his little "hobby." Now that hobby was threatening to break them up. Eva admitted defeat. She had worked all day at teaching Dodger that stealing was wrong, but he hadn't bought it. Whatever creep had taught him to do this had done too good a job.

It was time to go home. Maybe there she'd find some answers.

Eva opened the door and set her bags on the porch. Closing the door, she went back inside and called to Dodger.

"Let's do one last check upstairs and then we'll wait outside. C'mon!"

They went through all the rooms, making sure everything was picked up and put away.

The doorbell rang just as they came out of the bedroom.

Both Eva and Dodger jumped a mile.

Eva took Dodger's hand and stared down into the living room.

"It can't be the cab guy already," she whispered.

The bell rang again.

Eva dropped to the top step, with Dodger huddled beside her.

"Maybe if we ignore them, they'll go away."

No good. Someone gently knocked on the door.

"Hello?" someone called out. "Anybody there?"

Dodger jumped into Eva's lap. He wrapped his arms tightly around her neck and began shivering.

"You're shaking all over!" Eva whispered. "Don't be so scared."

Dodger just hugged Eva even more tightly. She got up slowly and cautiously edged down the stairs.

"Keep quiet," she warned Dodger in a soft voice. "We'll see who it is."

Clinging to each other, they reached the living room. Eva was just as scared as Dodger, although she wouldn't admit it. They crept to the curtained window near the front door. Careful not to make a sound, Eva drew back a corner of the curtain.

Staring directly at her was a monster with rotten teeth, an earring, and a bandanna!

Eva and Dodger both let out bloodcurdling screams.

Eva dropped the curtain and squeezed Dodger.

"It's the pirate!" she shouted.

CHAPTER
13

Open up!" the monster ordered. "I need to talk to you!"

Frozen with fear, Eva couldn't move. The Caribbean pirate who owned Dodger was standing inches away on the front porch. She had made him up whenever people asked where she'd gotten the monkey, but he was real. And he was scary and he wanted to take Dodger away.

She couldn't let that happen.

Thinking quickly, she yelled, "Dad! Dad! Come down here! Hurry! There's a man trying to get in!"

"I'm not trying to get in," the ugly pirate said through the window. "I only want to talk."

"Go away!"

"Get your father, girl."

"He's busy," Eva said.

The scary dark eyes of the pirate narrowed. "Or maybe he ain't there at all!"

In a panic, Eva and Dodger dashed up the stairs.

"We have to hide!" Eva whispered.

Down below she heard the front door rattle, then open.

"Mr. Boylan?" the pirate called.

He was inside the house!

Eva shot into her dad's bedroom as Dodger scurried under the bed.

"Oh, little girl!" the pirate called in a phony sweet voice. It didn't fool Eva. He meant to hurt them. She had to get Dodger to a safer hiding place.

Shorty crept into the living room, one eye out for the brat's father. A silver picture frame caught his attention. Without hesitating, he picked it up and slid it into the pocket of his large coat.

"Oh, little girl, don't be afraid," he whispered, creeping up the stairs. "I only want to talk with ya."

The upstairs hall was deserted. He couldn't

hear a peep. He went into the bedroom. The dresser held a good haul. Shorty helped himself to a gold ID bracelet, a watch, and a jeweled tie clip. Now it was time to collect the monkey. He walked out into the hall.

"Where are you, darlin'?" he called.

Eva and Dodger had climbed up into the attic, then pulled the trapdoor shut behind them. Now Eva was standing on a packing box, struggling to pull herself through the same porthole window Dodger had used to enter the house. Behind her Dodger pushed at her butt, helping her squeeze through the tight space.

Eva looked down and quickly shut her eyes. It was a long drop from the roof to the ground. But the evil pirate couldn't catch them. She wouldn't let him take Dodger away. Opening her eyes, she grabbed the tree branch closest to the window. She clung to it tightly, feeling it sway beneath her weight. She'd never make it down in one piece.

Dodger chattered softly behind her, then pushed her feet away from the porthole. Biting back a scream, Eva hung on to the swaying branch with all her might. Dodger popped up beside her and patted her arm. He showed

108

her a foothold. Closely following her monkey, Eva climbed down safely.

Running out of patience, Shorty searched the guest bedroom before discovering the attic trapdoor. That bratty girl wasn't going to get away with his monkey this time. Cursing under his breath, he grabbed a bathroom stepstool to reach the pull-down staircase.

Down below, Eva and Dodger had reached the ground safely. They raced to the porch to pick up her duffel bag and knapsack. Then Dodger ran across the street to the pirate's truck and trailer. While Eva kept an eye on the house, Dodger stood on the hitch between the motor home and the truck. First he pulled out the pin that held the safety chain. Then, chattering excitedly, he began pounding on the ball hitch. Eva helped him once she figured out what he was doing.

Suddenly a loud honking interrupted them, and the cab pulled up in front of the house. Frowning, Eva pushed Dodger into the knapsack and raced over to the cab.

The honking had attracted Shorty's attention. He poked his head out of the attic porthole window.

"Driver, wait!" he shouted.

Eva turned to wave up at the pirate and yelled, "'Bye, Dad! See you in a couple of weeks!"

She scrambled into the cab with her bags and ordered the driver to go.

"I don't take minors," the unfriendly-looking cab driver said. "You got money?"

Eva fumbled in the knapsack and pulled out a fat wad of bills. "See? Now go!"

The cab squealed away just as the front door opened and a red-faced, panting Shorty thundered out. Cursing, he dived into his truck and started the engine. That brat would not keep his monkey!

The cab went down Wellesley and approached the top of the steep hill at Seventeenth. Eva sat in the back of the cab, nervously glancing out the rear window. The pirate was right behind them and getting closer!

"Can't you go a little faster?" she pleaded with the cabby.

"How much faster?"

She threw the whole wad of bills into his lap.

"This much!"

Eva was thrown back in her seat as the

110

driver hit the gas. The cab slammed down the steep hill and went over a big bump. The truck did the same. But then a miracle happened.

Eva watched in amazed delight as the pirate's trailer broke free and rolled right past him on the hill! The cab turned left, but the runaway trailer and truck went straight, knocking over roadwork signs and smashing into a huge mound of dirt on a dead-end street. That put the pirate right in his place, Eva thought, cheering and whooping. Maybe luck was on their side, after all, and everything would turn out fine.

But her high spirits sank once she got home.

Tom Gregory opened the door of the apartment with a welcoming smile and took her duffel bag. "Hi. Where's Peter?"

"He, ah, you know, he was late for a date or something," she said, avoiding her stepdad's eyes. "Where's Mom?"

"With Jack at Megan's party. Did you have a nice weekend?"

About as nice as a pile of Dodger's used diapers.

"Great," she said.

Tom spotted something on the carpet. He picked it up and held it out to Eva.

"What's this?" he asked.

Eva stared in horror at a flashy brooch, one of the items Dodger had stolen in Venice. It must have fallen out of the knapsack.

"I don't know—how would I know?" Eva snapped. "It's not mine."

Tom gave her a strange look. "Okay."

Eva sighed. "I'm tired."

The tension of the weekend was starting to get to her. She had to escape to her room and be alone.

"Want to watch the ball game with me?" Tom offered. "Your Dodgers are playing the Pirates."

Dodgers. Pirates. That did it. Eva burst into tears.

"What did I say?" Tom asked, puzzled. "What's wrong?"

Eva grabbed her bags and slammed into the bedroom, leaving Tom with the stolen brooch and a worried expression. His police station had been working on a recent string of petty thefts in the area, and many of them involved stolen jewelry.

Tom stared down at the brooch, then in the direction of Eva's bedroom. He didn't like what he was thinking.

CHAPTER
14

Shorty had bounced back and gotten a lead.

Now he was smiling at a well-dressed elderly couple, Harold and Kaye Weller. The Wellers had noticed one of Shorty's posters at the park and had paged him on his beeper. They had information about a missing monkey, they told him, and agreed to meet him in the park. As soon as the tow-truck guys had reattached his motor home to his pickup, Shorty had practically flown to the meeting. He hadn't had time to clean up or change.

The Wellers took one look at his dirty, unshaven face and nervously huddled together.

"You don't look like a doctor," Kaye Weller said in a squeak.

Shorty smoothed down his hair and tried to act the part.

"What can I tell you, I've been in surgery all night. I can't rest till I find my monkey."

"Now, we can't be sure it was your monkey we saw," Harold Weller said. "First time was right here in the park, with a little girl. Same day Mother lost her earring and I lost my wallet."

Shorty nearly danced a jig. "Sounds like it could be my monkey. Do you know where the girl lives?"

"I'm afraid we don't," Kaye Weller said.

Shorty's face fell. "You said you saw the monkey the 'first time.' When was the second time?"

Harold Weller said the magic words. "Oh, over at the pet shop." He gave Shorty the address.

Shorty flashed a rotten-toothed smile that made the Wellers wince. Tomorrow he'd steal the monkey, and no pint-size, smart-mouthed brat was going to stop him!

Eva dropped off Dodger at the pet shop on Monday morning.

"Don't let Dodger near the cash register!" she warned Annie before she left. "I'll explain later!"

Boy, would she have a lot of explaining to do, Eva thought as she headed toward school, explaining to a lot of people, and she dreaded it.

Eva couldn't concentrate in school all morning. Thoughts of Dodger kept running through her head. She had to do something about her pickpocket pet, but she didn't know what. Maybe Christine, her teacher, could help.

"I did something I thought was okay," Eva told her teacher at recess. "Only it turned out not to be okay, and now it's out of control. I want to undo it, but I don't know how."

Christine listened, then said, "No matter what you've done, Eva, you have to tell your parents. Go to your mom, talk to her. Don't be afraid."

Eva looked up, sure that Christine could see how scared she was. "I've been lying too much."

"Then telling the truth is the only way to make things better," Christine said. "And you know what? It'll make you feel better after you've told them."

Eva nodded slowly. Right after school she'd go pick up Dodger and then face her parents.

But later, when Eva got to the pet shop, a Closed sign was hanging on the door. She tried the door, and it opened, but no Annie greeted her. A man she had never seen before sat at the register, nervously snapping rubber bands. When he saw Eva, he jumped a foot in the air and pointed at the door.

"Store's closed. You can't come in."

"Who are you?" Eva asked.

"I'm from the laundromat next door," the man said.

This wasn't making any sense. "Where's Annie?"

"She's—she's not here, she had to go to the police station. A bit of an emergency, actually."

"What happened?" Eva cried. "Is she all right?"

Oh no, if Annie was gone . . . Eva wheeled around to check on Dodger's cage. It was empty.

"Where's my monkey?" Eva demanded. There was a tight feeling in her stomach.

"Oh dear, I don't know anything about a monkey," the man twittered nervously.

116

"Annie was keeping my monkey for me!" Eva cried.

"All I know is that some horrible man came in and stole some things, got her terribly upset, and she had to run off and report it to the police."

Tears rolled down Eva's face. The absolutely worst thing in the world had happened.

"The pirate!" she sobbed. "He found us! Now he's stolen my poor little Dodger, and I'll never see him again!"

Shorty was floating on air.

He had gotten his monkey back, and now he and Drake and Charlie were sitting in the fancy reception area of some office, waiting to see the boss. The two goons and Shorty sat on a black leather sofa. Shorty's son, Mark, was perched on the edge of a coffee table and held on to Dodger. Shorty grinned at his son and his monkey, but neither one grinned back. Mark had a scowl on his face, and the monkey wriggled in his arms. It looked to Shorty as though the two wanted to escape.

Shorty took the monkey out of his son's arms.

"Where's my money?" Mark demanded.

"Later, kid." Shorty brushed him off. "Go back to the car. I don't need you right now."

Mark jumped up and left quickly.

Shorty turned to Drake. For a change the goon was beaming at him.

"This is it, Shorty, one step away from the big score." Drake looked at Charlie. "Amigo, let's show him the demo loot."

Charlie nodded and pulled out a handful of glittering junk jewelry. Seeing it, Dodger hopped out of Shorty's arms and slapped Charlie's hand with one of the magazines on the table.

Charlie made a face and looked at Drake. "Hey! Why did he do that?"

Shorty motioned Dodger over. He pulled out an empty drawstring purse and handed it to the monkey. Dodger refused to take it and shook his head. Shorty stared in disbelief. What was going on? His monkey always jumped on the drawstring purses!

"Come on, this ain't the time for joking around," Shorty pleaded.

He tried to give Dodger the purse again, but the monkey firmly pushed his hand away. For one of the few times in his life, Shorty was speechless.

118

"I don't get it, Drake," Charlie said.

Drake didn't get it, either.

Desperate now, Shorty tried another idea.

"You guys got a wallet? Give me a wallet."

Charlie pulled out his wallet and handed it to Shorty. As Shorty took it, Dodger hopped between the two men. He grabbed the billfold and returned it to Charlie. Drake made a hissing sound and grabbed Shorty but released him when a grim-faced assistant came out of the boss's office.

"He's ready for you guys," the assistant announced.

"In a second," Drake said.

"Now, Drake!" the assistant ordered. "Come on, Charlie."

Charlie followed the assistant into the office. A rattled-looking Drake glared back at Shorty. He pointed a don't-mess-with-me finger at him.

"Don't move," Drake commanded.

Drake entered the boss's office like a bad kid having to visit the principal.

Shorty didn't need to be whacked over the head to know he was in trouble. They *all* were, but him most of all. He grabbed a

119

wiggling Dodger and took off. Now he had to beat feet to escape from the two goons. As he ran, he wondered what the girl had done to his monkey. He ground his teeth, thinking of ways to get even with the little brat if he ever found her again.

CHAPTER
15

Eva quietly slipped in the front door of the Gregory apartment and then hesitated in the hall. Losing Dodger had hurt like crazy, and now she had to tell her mother and Tom everything. This was turning out to be the worst day of her life.

Walking in slow motion, feeling her knees wobble, Eva headed for her parents' bedroom. She could hear them inside, talking. From the sound of their conversation, they weren't turning cartwheels, either.

Eva screwed up her courage and opened the door. Her mom was sitting on the bed, her eyes red and swollen. A grim-faced Tom stood behind her.

"Mom, I want to talk to you," Eva began. "I'm in such big trouble. . . ."

"You bet you are," Tom interrupted. He held out Eva's jewelry box, crammed to the top with jewelry, wallets, tie clips, and money.

Amy turned shocked eyes on Eva. "Tom found this in your room! Eva, how could you have done this? Why?"

Eva brought her hands to her face and sighed. Dodger up to his old tricks again. If only she had known . . .

"I've never seen this stuff before, Mom. I didn't steal anything. It's my monkey. My monkey did it."

Tom stared at her. "Your monkey? What monkey?"

"He jumped down on me in the park one day! I've had him for over a month."

"What are you talking about?" Amy cried. "We've never seen any monkey."

"Because I've been hiding him!" Eva insisted. "And just the other day I found out that he steals like a maniac! And today I went to pick him up at the pet shop, and the pirate who trained him had taken him back! My poor Dodger . . . I was trying to make him stop stealing, but now . . ."

Eva broke off, afraid she'd start to cry. Tom

and Amy didn't say a word. Their shocked, disbelieving faces said it all.

Tom was a police lieutenant. Maybe he could get some officers to search the neighborhood for Dodger. Eva turned to him.

"Tom, you've got to help me find him!"

But her stepdad was frowning and shaking his head.

"For pete's sake, Eva, if you're going to make up a lie—"

"But it's the truth!" Eva shouted.

"No!" cried Amy.

Neither of them believed her, Eva realized. Not Tom, who always listened to her side of the story, and not even her mom.

Tom moved to the phone.

"Okay, let's call the pet shop."

"No, wait," Eva said. "The thing is, the man who's there now doesn't know about my monkey, because Annie had to leave after the pirate, and—"

"That's enough, just stop it!" her mom said. She began to cry. "How could you steal from me!"

Eva couldn't get a word out. How could her mom think such a horrible thing?

"I didn't, Mommy," Eva said quietly.

Tom stepped forward. "Her antique pin,

her ring. They're not in here. Where are they?"

Tom was looking at her as if she were a suspect at the station or something. Eva shook her head, fighting back tears. The only thing she cared about was Dodger, and he was gone forever.

Dodger was locked inside the trailer's bathroom. Shorty had been furious with him when he refused to steal the wallet from the man in the office. He had grabbed Dodger and run to the waiting truck and trailer, screaming bad things the entire time. Then he'd dumped him inside the cramped, smelly bathroom and locked the door. The truck was moving now, heading somewhere. Probably back to Venice Beach. Dodger didn't want to go there. He wanted to be with the girl.

Dodger threw himself against the bathroom door. The lock held. He looked up at the skylight. Scampering up the wall, he began trying to unlatch the skylight.

In the cab of the truck, an angry Shorty was driving. Mark sat squeezed as far away from him as possible. Shorty thought about the monkey at the boss's office and how he'd refused to steal. Shorty Kohn had been made to look like a monkey! It was all that girl's fault.

"What did she do to him?" Shorty shouted, banging his fist on the dashboard. "Years of training, wrecked!"

If he ever saw that tiny brat again . . .

His fingers tightened on the steering wheel.

They were still questioning Eva when Tessa brought Jack home.

Tom asked Eva the same stupid questions, and she gave him the same honest answers. Only no one believed her. Eva paced around the room, biting her nails.

Only Jack seemed happy. Her brother sat in front of the TV, watching a children's program. Eva wished she could join him and tune out this mess.

Now Tom started in on Tessa. He asked if she knew about Eva's pet.

"Of course I never saw a monkey," Tessa said.

"Because I kept him hidden in my knapsack!" Eva shouted, for perhaps the fiftieth time. She could shout it fifty more times, and no one would believe her. She had hidden Dodger *too* well, Eva thought.

The doorbell rang.

Amy hurried out to open the door. Peter Boylan rushed in, then stopped when he saw how upset Amy was.

"Peter!" Amy cried. "I'm glad you're here. Do you know anything about this?"

Peter was confused. "About what? I was in the neighborhood doing errands, and since I missed Eva on the weekend—"

Amy whipped around. "What do you mean 'missed' her?"

"Amy, I was flying all over Canada last weekend. What happened?"

Amy and Peter entered the living room together.

Eva knew she was in even more trouble the minute she saw her father. She jammed her hands into her pockets to stop them from shaking.

"Uh-oh. Dad."

Amy lost control. She turned on Eva and screamed, "Where were you this weekend while your father was *out of town?*"

"At his house," Eva said in an embarrassed whisper.

"What?" Peter cried. "Were you down at my house when I got robbed?"

Tom stepped forward. "She stole from you, too?"

"Eva did?" Peter's eyes bugged out.

"How could you have gone to your father's by yourself!" Amy yelled at Eva. "What were you thinking?"

"I just needed time alone with my monkey."

"What monkey?" Peter asked, completely confused.

Amy turned to him. "She's been stealing all over town, and now she's trying to blame it on some imaginary, invisible monkey!"

"I'm telling you, he's real!" Eva shouted.

Amy had had it. "Go to your room."

"But, Mom—"

"Go and stay there until you're ready to tell us *the truth!*"

Eva looked up at all the unbelieving faces. Didn't anyone think she was being honest? Their faces said no.

With a slump in her shoulders, Eva turned and headed for her bedroom.

CHAPTER
16

Shorty was driving past the park where he had met the Wellers. This had to be the little girl's neighborhood. He gritted his teeth, thinking about her. It would take weeks, *months* to retrain his monkey, but he'd do it. Starting tonight, the monkey was in for his first lesson. Shorty muttered to himself as he stopped at a light next to an eighteen-wheeler truck.

Inside the trailer bathroom, Dodger finally kicked open the skylight hatch. He scrambled to the roof of the trailer and looked around. There was Eva's park! They were close to her building. Dodger didn't wait. He jumped from the trailer roof into the open passenger window of a big truck. He jumped across the two startled men and darted out the driver's-side window. Dodger took off across the street.

The driver of the eighteen-wheeler pulled up next to Shorty's truck.

"Hey, your monkey jumped off!" the driver shouted.

Shorty whipped his head around. His monkey was sprinting toward the park! With a squeal of tires, Shorty turned the truck and trailer around. No way would he lose the monkey again!

Eva was searching her room for any sign or proof that Dodger had been there. How could the place be so spotless? So empty of her monkey? It was as if Dodger had never existed.

Jack came in and toddled up to her.

"Da?"

Eva knew he was looking for his friend. He missed Dodger, too.

Tears threatened to spill. She got down on her knees.

"Eva sad, Jack," she said, hugging her brother. "Dodger gone, all gone."

Eva's best friend, Katie, was running down the field during soccer practice. Her team had the ball, and she motioned for one of her friends to pass it to her.

"Here, Gus!" she shouted. "I'm open!"

A movement overhead caught Katie's attention. Her mouth dropped open. No, it couldn't be! Only this past weekend Eva had shown her the "surprise," and now here was the surprise on the soccer field. Eva's pet monkey must have escaped.

Katie stared so hard at the racing monkey that she missed the soccer ball. It rolled past her, straight into the path of the opposite team. While Gus and her teammates yelled at her, Katie dashed off the field. She had to call Eva to tell her the monkey was in the park.

Eighteen-month-old Jack knew all about the monkey, but no one would listen. He showed his Baby Ben book to Tessa and pointed to a picture of a monkey. Tessa shrugged and smiled and made nice noises. She didn't understand. Jack kept pointing to the picture.

Behind them, Amy, Tom, and Peter sat on the sofa in the living room, huddled in a conference. They were still discussing Eva's weekend.

"Two days out there?" Amy was saying with

a worried frown. "We're lucky she wasn't kidnapped or killed."

"This doesn't make sense," Peter stated.

It didn't make sense because no one believed her story about Dodger, Eva thought. She had crept out of her bedroom and was listening in on the grown-ups' conversation. She hugged the wall and kept extremely still.

"Eva has always been so honest," her father was saying. "I don't think she's ever lied to us before, do you?"

Amy agreed. "It's just not like her. I don't believe she's a thief, and she certainly wouldn't steal from me."

"I've got the evidence," Tom said. "But it doesn't add up for me, either."

They were sticking up for her! Eva's spirits lifted. She tiptoed back into her room and sat at the desk, thinking.

Tom, Amy, and Peter continued talking in the living room, trying to make sense of the situation.

"I just find this 'monkey' very hard to believe," Amy said with a shake of her head.

The phone rang. Tessa answered it.

"Hello . . . Katie?"

Amy turned around and raised an eyebrow.

131

Tessa got the message and said, "Katie, listen to me. Is it true that Eva has a monkey?"

From a pay phone near the soccer field, Katie thought hard and fast. She didn't want to lie, but a sworn promise to a friend was sacred. She raised her free hand and crossed her fingers.

"Monkey? No way, she would have told me. No, I swear. Can I speak to her? Please, Tessa?"

Tessa stared at Amy and shook her head. No one had seen this invisible monkey, not even Eva's closest friend.

Tessa left the living room and headed for Eva's bedroom with the phone.

"Katie for you."

Eva turned around, her face alight. "Ask her, she knows! She's seen my monkey!"

"I already did," Tessa said. "She has no idea what you're talking about."

Tessa handed Eva the phone and left.

Eva said hello, then jumped up at what Katie told her. After her friend hung up, Eva grabbed a piece of paper and began to write.

Dodger was jumping too, and hopping and hooting. He was trying to cross the street. Cars beeped and screeched to a stop when

Dodger darted through. Only a few more blocks and he'd be safe, out of Shorty's hands forever.

Luckily, Dodger didn't turn around.

Shorty and Mark had pulled up next to the park and gotten out of the truck. Shorty pointed one way, then the other. Mark nodded, and they headed off in opposite directions.

Amy, Tom, and Peter were still in conference in the Gregory living room.

"We need to decide how we're going to handle this," Tom said. "You have to try to get to the root of the problem. I see it happen all the time: A kid starts lying, does something wrong, next thing you know, the parents call us to report a runaway."

Unseen by everyone, Eva had tiptoed through the hall and left the apartment. Bursting out of the lobby, she hit the sidewalk and took off across the street to the park.

CHAPTER
17

At the exact same moment that Eva raced to the park, Dodger reached the apartment building. He scampered up the tree and nimbly hopped into the Gregorys' bathroom window. Home again!

Dodger raced across the hall and into Eva's room. She wasn't there. Before he could look for her, he heard noises. Dodger scooted under the bed. He peeked out from beneath the fringed coverlet.

The door opened and Jack wobbled in, followed by Tessa. Tessa called for Eva, then rushed into the bathroom. While she was gone, Dodger watched Jack walk around the bedroom. Dodger wanted to play with his little friend, but he knew that Tessa shouldn't see him. He'd have to wait.

Tessa came out, then grabbed a piece of paper from Eva's desk. She read it, looking sad and worried. Then she left, leaving Jack behind.

Two seconds later Dodger scooted out from underneath the bed.

Jack beamed a hundred-watt smile at his furry friend.

"Daaa!"

Dodger sat down near Jack, cooing back at him, waiting for Eva to return.

In the living room, Tessa handed Eva's note to Amy.

There was a tense silence as Amy read the note aloud to Peter and Tom:

"To Mom, Dad, and Tom: I love you very much. Katie just told me she saw my monkey in the park. I have to go rescue him. *P.S.*—This is not a lie. I swear. I'll never lie again, and I'll never keep a secret from you guys again."

Amy looked first at Tom, then at Peter. Their daughter had run off to the park to rescue her invisible monkey. The situation was getting out of hand. Amy stared down at the note in a daze.

Jack walked in and tugged at her sleeve.

"Not now," Amy said.

But Jack continued pointing his finger at Eva's room and making nonsense babbling sounds. He pulled at Amy's hand.

Amy was still staring at the letter. She barely glanced down at Jack. "Not now, Jack! Please!"

Jack refused to give up. He swung her hand and jabbered. Worn down by her son's non-stop babble and excitement, Amy followed Jack into Eva's bedroom. It was empty.

"What, what?" Amy asked impatiently.

Jack looked around, then made his "all gone!" wave.

"I know she's gone," Amy said sadly. "I have to go look for her."

She started to walk out when she heard Jack say, "M-m-m . . . mo-kky!"

That stopped Amy cold. She turned in disbelief.

"What did you say?"

Jack took a deep breath. "Mon-key!"

It came out even clearer this time, and he pointed to the bed.

136

"Peter! Tom! Hurry!" Amy called.

She knelt by Jack, who was still pointing to the bed. The two men and Tessa rushed in.

"Shh," Amy proudly whispered. "He's saying his first word."

Peter raised an eyebrow. "Big deal, he's almost two."

"Monkey! Monkey!" Jack nearly jumped up and down with excitement.

Tom, Peter, and Tessa exchanged looks.

"Don't you think he's trying to tell us something?" Amy insisted. "That a monkey was here, and he saw it?"

Peter went to the bed and pulled a stuffed monkey off the cover.

"This is what he's trying to tell us," he said. He held the toy out to Jack. "Here's your monkey. Right, Jack?"

Jack shook his head. He dropped to all fours and started to crawl under the bed.

Suddenly his body was sucked in by some unseen force!

Amy shrieked as Tom rushed over. He grabbed hold of Jack's legs and tugged him back out. Jack reappeared—holding Dodger by the ankles!

Four shocked, bug-eyed faces stared at this sight.

137

"Amazing! There *is* a monkey!" Amy said, and she burst out laughing. "She was telling the truth!"

Jack nodded his head and beamed. He stuck his hand on Dodger's head.

The grown-ups couldn't stop talking about the monkey until Peter came to his senses.

"Come on," he said. "Let's go find Eva."

Eva was searching for Dodger.

Katie had waited for her friend by the soccer field and pointed out where she had last seen Dodger. Then Katie's impatient nanny had whisked Katie away.

Eva had to search the park alone, but she wasn't scared. She was too excited and happy. She thought the evil pirate had stolen Dodger away forever, but Dodger had managed to escape. He was probably looking for her right this very minute!

"Dodger!" Eva called loudly. "Dodger!"

She approached the large tree where Dodger had first dropped in her path. Maybe, just maybe, he'd be waiting for her here. Eva raced around the tree—and ran smack into the pirate!

She tried to run, but he grabbed her shoulders.

"What have you done to my monkey, sweetheart?" His smile was phony, his eyes dangerous.

Eva twisted in his grasp. "He's not your monkey anymore! He ran away from you because he hates you! He came to me!"

The pirate snorted. "He came to you just 'cause he likes kids! He belongs to my son, Mark, who's around here somewheres, looking like crazy for his monkey. You stealed it from him. Now, you don't want to break this poor kid's heart, do you?"

"I don't believe you!" Eva cried. "Liar!"

The pirate's face turned bright red with rage. "What did you do to my monkey? You brainwashed him! He doesn't steal anymore!"

Eva stood still in shock. "Are you serious?"

"That's right. And don't pretend you ain't did it! Don't you lie to me, girl!"

"I've quit lying!" Eva declared. "And I'm glad he doesn't steal anymore! Well done, Dodger!"

Eva aimed a kick at the pirate's legs, but he wouldn't let go.

"My monkey's name is Fingers, not Dodger!" he snarled. "I hate the Dodgers!"

CHAPTER
18

Eva's parents couldn't find her.

Amy and Peter, with Tom carrying Dodger, were combing the park with little success. Tom had even gotten a police car to follow them. Now Tom stopped the car and talked to one of the two uniformed officers. He put Dodger down.

When he straightened up, he heard Peter yell, "The monkey's getting away!"

"Don't lose sight of him!" Tom shouted.

Tom, Amy, and Peter chased Dodger but lost him in a thick grove of trees.

KABOOM! A gunshot rang out.

Tom immediately reached for his holster.

"My gun!" Tom cried. "He's got my gun!"

The three took off in the direction of the shot, praying that nothing bad had happened.

Shorty prayed the same thing.

Somehow his monkey had gotten hold of a gun and squeezed off a shot. It had missed him by miles. Next time he might not be so lucky. Shorty was frozen with fear but still wouldn't release Eva.

"He came to rescue me!" Eva cried proudly.

"Where'd you get that gun?" Shorty demanded. "Drop it!"

He glowered at the monkey. The monkey had always obeyed him before, but not any longer. The furry little monster pointed the gun straight at him. Shorty ducked behind a tree in fright. Eva wiggled out of his hold and ran behind Dodger.

"Come on, baby, drop it and run!" she urged Dodger.

Dodger placed furry fingers on the trigger.

"Easy now, Fingers!" Shorty pleaded nervously. "Steady there . . ."

Shorty leapt back as Dodger squeezed off another shot. This one hit the ground next to Shorty.

Peter, Tom, and Amy raced out from between the trees, followed by the police car.

"Eva! We're here!" Amy cried.

When he heard her voice, Dodger dropped the gun. This was Shorty's chance, and he ran. Tom took off after him.

"Momma!" Eva shouted.

Amy and Peter ran to her and pulled her into a three-way hug. Dodger wanted it *four*-way. He scampered among them all and worked his way in.

"I'm sorry!" Eva said. "I'm so sorry about everything."

Amy squeezed her tightly. "Thank goodness you're safe, sweetheart."

"And thank goodness this monkey exists!" Peter added, grinning down at Dodger.

I could kill that monkey! Shorty was thinking as he raced through the park. Just another few yards and he'd reach his trailer. He'd had tight brushes with the law before, but he'd always gotten away. The trailer was so close. . . .

A long black limo pulled up next to the trailer.

Charlie and Drake got out.

Seeing them, Shorty skidded to a halt. This was *worse* than the law. He froze to the spot.

"Get in the car," Drake said.

"Get in the car!" Charlie echoed.

Tom popped up behind Shorty, trailed by the police car.

"Okay, pal!" Tom said. "You're under arrest!"

Shorty turned to Tom with a grateful sigh. "Thank you!"

Saved—by the police. Shorty offered a mocking wave to the two goons before he jogged toward Tom.

"These men are killers, they want to hurt me!"

Drake and Charlie disappeared into the limo. With tires squealing, they drove off.

Tom handcuffed Shorty. One of the police officers frisked him and found a drawstring purse. Tom recited Shorty's Miranda rights as the officer checked the contents of the purse.

"Lieutenant," the officer said, "check this out."

He held out a handful of money, wallets, and jewelry. Tom immediately recognized Amy's antique diamond pin and ring among the stolen items. Astounded but happy, he gave Shorty a big hug. Wait until Amy saw this!

143

A short distance away, Eva was hugging Dodger and pleading with Amy and Peter.

"He doesn't steal anymore!" she cried. "The pirate even said so. Ask him."

Tom came trotting up with a huge grin and a surprise for Amy. Amy examined the jewelry with a unbelieving smile.

"My— How?" she stuttered. "This is great!"

Dodger jumped into Tom's arms and stroked his face as if to say "I agree!"

Everyone laughed.

But Eva stared at Tom with rounded eyes. Didn't anyone realize? Tom was inches away from animal fur and—

"Hey, Tom's not sneezing!" she shouted.

"He's been with us so long, I probably got used to him," Tom said, stroking Dodger's fur.

Dodger jumped back into Eva's arms. Now that Tom was no longer bothered by his allergy, Eva thought that maybe Dodger could be her pet.

"Can I keep him?" Eva pleaded. "Please? Now you know how responsible I can be—I took care of him so good, you didn't even know I had him!"

"She's got a point," Peter muttered to Amy.

"Yeah, I do, I really do."

"It's fine with me," Tom agreed. He winked at Eva. "I have to take that guy in. See you later, kiddo."

As soon as Tom had left, Eva turned to her mom.

"So what do you say? Can I keep him? Can I?"

But before Amy could answer, Eva spotted something that made her heart sink. It was a boy about ten or eleven wearing a baseball cap, standing fifty yards away by a tree. He was watching what was going on with a funny expression on his face.

The pirate really did have a son. He hadn't been lying.

And that boy probably loved Dodger as much as she did.

Dodger didn't belong to her. He belonged to the boy.

Clutching the monkey, Eva walked super slowly toward the boy. When she was about ten yards away, she stopped. He hadn't said a word or moved a muscle the entire time.

Tears filled Eva's eyes as she stared down at Dodger.

"He's your daddy, isn't he?"

Dodger looked at the boy.

Eva could barely speak. "I love him a lot, you know?"

"Who cares?" the boy said in a nasty voice. "He belongs to me."

Eva hesitated, dreading the horrible, heart-breaking moment of letting Dodger go. As she did, the boy reached into his pocket and pulled something out.

The boy kneeled down and extended a cupped hand to Dodger. Eva couldn't see what he was holding.

Whatever it was, it attracted Dodger's attention. He sniffed the air, then ran across to the boy.

Dodger had chosen. There was nothing Eva could do.

Fighting back tears, Eva slowly got up and walked back to Amy and Peter. She took their hands.

"What happened?" her mom asked.

"That's Dodger's real dad," Eva whispered. "I let Dodger choose, and he decided to go live with him. Can we go home now?"

Amy nodded sympathetically and gave her a hug. They began walking out of the park.

"Maybe you can work something out,"

Peter suggested. "A joint-custody agreement . . ."

Eva walked slowly between them, head down, feeling her heart break. She tried to put on a brave front so she wouldn't cry.

"Now I know why he liked my hat," she said softly, talking to herself. "I mean, I understand. It's only fair, Dodger was his first. If I lost him, I'd sure want somebody to give him back to me."

The brave front collapsed. Eva sobbed openly, feeling the pain.

"I just want Dodger to be happy," she said. "I'm going to think of him and love him for the rest of my life."

CHAPTER
19

But Dodger wasn't happy at all.

He had eaten the dead tree lizard out of Mark's hand, but now he wanted to return to Eva. Only something was stopping him—the leash Mark had snapped on him. Struggling with the collar, Dodger found and then unhooked the clasp. He turned and waved goodbye to Mark before he scampered away.

Could he catch up to Eva in time?

He raced across the grass, screeching loudly.

Eva and her parents were up ahead. As soon as she heard Dodger's cry, she whipped around and caught him in midjump! He landed on her neck and hugged her tight. Screaming for joy, Eva hugged him back even harder. Dodger had chosen her, and they'd never be parted again.

Eva was excited and proud.

Nervous too, but mostly proud.

Today was a red-letter day for her, and she wanted it to go perfectly.

She was in her classroom at school, standing by the open door. All eyes in the room were focused on her. Soon they'd see something that would *really* make them sit up and take notice.

Eva tried to wave in her special guest from outside the hall.

"C'mon, don't be afraid," she said in an encouraging voice. "This is our big day!"

She held her breath and then smiled as Jack walked in.

Nervously, he gazed around at all the strange faces.

Eva took his hand and walked him to the front of the room. Dodger was already at his seat by Christine's desk, sitting quietly and wearing a red cap.

Jack broke into a huge grin and pointed at Dodger.

"E-va . . . mon-key."

Everyone in the class burst into warm laughter.

Eva knelt down by her brother, her face glowing with pride.

She pointed at Jack.

"E-va . . . Jack!"

Eva hugged and squeezed him as Jack hugged her back. She kissed him on the forehead and got up. Then she waved at Dodger, who immediately hopped down to join them.

Standing in the middle, Eva took Jack's hand on one side and Dodger's hand on the other. She took a deep breath and smiled proudly and confidently at her teacher.

"I'm ready for my show-and-tell," she said.

All the kids applauded.

Eva bowed.

Jack smiled.

And Dodger tipped his hat.

About the Author

ELLEN LEROE has loved cooking up tales of mystery and magic ever since she wrote her first book, *Skull and Dagger Island*, when she was nine years old. She has authored novels for teenagers and younger readers featuring her favorite subjects: poltergeists, ghosts, and cupids—not to mention a mean mechanical robot.

Born in East Orange, New Jersey, she now lives in San Francisco, California, where she enjoys views of the Bay Bridge and Alcatraz Prison. She has no plans to move, although the earth moves her quite often, the latest experience being the 7.1 earthquake in 1989.

Ellen Leroe gets many of her ideas for her books from the diaries she wrote from the fifth grade all the way through college. Other inspirations come from her niece and two nephews, who live close by and read all her stories.

In addition to writing, Ms. Leroe reads books (about four a week), and especially loves those she calls "high on the Creepmeter of Scare." She has traveled all over Europe and now enjoys aerobics, conversation with good friends at local coffee shops, and the theater—and a good horror movie or two.

Ms. Leroe is the author of *H.O.W.L. High*, *Heebie-Jeebies at H.O.W.L. High*, and *H.O.W.L. High Goes Bats!* All available from Minstrel Books.